A Forbidden Taking

AARONS KISS SERIES BOOK 11

KATHI S. BARTON

This is a work of fiction. Names, characters, places, and incidents are products of the author's imagination or are used fictitiously and are not to be construed as real. Any resemblance to actual events, locations, organizations, or person, living or dead, is entirely coincidental.

WCP

World Castle Publishing
Pensacola, Florida

Copyright © Kathi S. Barton 2013
ISBN: 9781938961762
First Edition World Castle Publishing January 1, 2013
http://www.worldcastlepublishing.com

Cover: Karen Fuller
Photos: Shutterstock
Editor: Brieanna Robertson

Chapter 1

Megan moved toward her car. She was exhausted and her head hurt. Rubbing her forehead with her finger tips she staggered slightly when she bumped into a parked car. Laughing slightly to herself she continued on until she could see her car.

Megan Reed was only a few short days from getting her results back from her state exams, then she'd be a full fledged doctor. Nine years waiting for this day and she was almost too tired to be happy. Grinning as she came upon her car, she rubbed her hand over the trunk and thought about what kind of car she would buy when she had the money. A fast back, she decided, and maybe a—

The noise came out of nowhere. It was a low, keening sound that made her want to run and hide. Looking around she couldn't see anything, but instinctively she knew she wasn't alone. Moving to the door she pulled out her keys and kept darting her gaze around looking for it, for something. When the shadow fell across her face she nearly screamed out loud, her hand going to her throat before she realized she knew the person.

"Alfred, you scared the life out of me," she said as she leaned against the car. "Where have you been lately? I haven't seen you in weeks."

Alfred Deveron stared at her. She looked around for his car and wasn't surprised that it was still in the same place it had been for the last two weeks. She'd heard rumors that he'd gone off with one of his women, but who knew with this man? He was as strange as they came. She looked back at him and noticed he looked ill.

"Alfred?"

"I'm sorry, Megan. I'm hungry. I'm really sorry." She started to get a little scared when he came toward her.

"That's okay. I'll…maybe I can get you something at the local diner. My treat. You can meet me there."

She knew as sure as she was standing there that as soon as he stepped away she was out of there. Alfred didn't look right. He looked…well, he looked dead. Megan started fumbling for the door handle and was startled when Alfred was suddenly right there, his hand gripping hers so tightly that she was sure he'd break bones if he kept it up.

"Alfred, you're hurting me. Let go of my hand or I'll call security. And step back. You're crowding—"

"I'm sorry, Megan. I wish I could do this differently, but I'm so hungry. So very hungry. And it only hurts for a little while, I promise."

He was too close now, much too close for her to get away, and incredibly strong. She'd never realized that he was so strong before. She started to struggle and pull away, but he simply wrapped his arm around her waist, trapping her arms and lifting her off the ground. Before she could scream or yell, he clasped his other hand over her mouth. She felt her lip burst from the pressure. He tightened his grip on her and suddenly—holy shit, they were flying.

Crying now, she screamed around his hand. Megan was afraid to struggle much, afraid that he would drop her and she'd die. When he started to nuzzle her neck, licking and nipping at her, she thought she would be sick. He smelled of old blood and death. Crying harder, she was startled when the ground was suddenly under her feet.

"You have to know that I'm sorry. I'm just so hungry." He licked her throat again and then pulled back to look at her.

His eyes were red. Not the bloodshot kind of a person who'd been crying a lot or had been drinking, but a blood red. The whites of his eyes were red. And his mouth. Screaming again, she looked at his teeth. He had…he had fucking fangs. When he licked her this time she really fought him, trying to get away. When she felt a rib break, she nearly passed out from the pain. Pausing slightly was all the encouragement he needed, apparently.

With another, "I'm so sorry," Alfred bit her. His teeth, his fangs, sank into her deep.

Her screams were ringing in her head. Now she was sick; her belly was churning over and over until she felt herself grow weak. When the colors started to fade from the trees around her and the grass became gray as well, she felt her knees grow wobbly then she drifted off. Her last thought was that she would never know what her results were.

~~~

The sun was close to setting, she thought, and Megan needed to move. Her body was sore and achy from lying in a cramped place for so long. She stretched and moved to open the way out. This was the part she hated more than anything, the not knowing.

She didn't know anything really. All this time and all she knew was that she was a monster. A horrible monster who wished every day that she could have died that day sixteen months ago. Testing the light coming in she was relieved to find it was indeed dark out and moved the seat out of the way and then moved out of her trunk.

She crawled out of the back seat and was standing up when the first wave of hunger hit her. Looking around she could see a couple of people milling around, and the sound of their hearts beating nearly drove her to slide back into her hidey hole.

That was the second thing she hated. Everything was too much. The sounds were too loud, the colors too bright, and the smells…some days she wanted bury her head in a gas mask to keep the smells away. She held onto the handle of her car trying to keep herself from going to them, the warm blooded people who would feed her.

Megan hated this part of herself too. The need to drink blood. The need to feed herself on the blood of others was sickening to her. She had tried not drinking from anyone, but that had been a mistake. She'd killed that man that one time and had vowed never to do that again. Now she fed nightly, or as close to that as she could. She wouldn't put herself in a predicament like that again. She started toward the two men standing next to the fire in the large can near the water.

"Cold, huh?" She grinned at them and hoped that her fangs wouldn't show.

She didn't know how they just knew to drop like they did. Sometimes when she was excited they just popped out. She tried to control them, but had only made it worse by thinking about them. Since they didn't run off she figured she was all right.

"Sure is. Huddle up closer, girl. You don't got enough meat on your bones to be standing around without a jacket on. You should go down to the shelter. They'll give you a nice fleece."

Megan looked down. She'd forgotten about a coat. The truth was, she didn't feel the cold like others did. Most of the time she was barefooted and would only wear shoes when someone would point it out to her. She moved closer to the fire and began rubbing her hands together.

Moving slightly closer to the man nearest to her she turned her body so that it looked as if she was seeking warmth from him. The other man couldn't really see her or what she was doing, but he did move up behind her other side and seemed to be sheltering her from the worst of the wind. She nearly cried out for them not to be nice to her, she was a monster, but she was hungry and kept quiet.

When she nuzzled up to his throat, she licked the area. The man, nearly twice her age, moaned in response. Before he could say anything she bit down. She was as gentle as she could be, but he still jerked a little. Soon he wasn't moving away, but turning so that his body was bumping hard against her thigh.

She'd learned that the first time she'd had to feed. Men got some sort of sexual release from her biting them. The first several times she'd felt them come in their pants she'd been sickened more by it. But soon she realized that if they got pleasure from this they didn't fight her as much. At least the older men didn't. She'd learned the hard way to keep away from the younger men. She was sealing up the wound when she felt someone coming.

Megan didn't move much, but her body was ready. She leaned into the second man, quicker now, and bit him as well. She never drank much, just a few swallows, but it was enough to get her through the night before she had to seek others out.

She saw the man in the shadows. He was just beyond the light of the fire, but with her powerful sight she could make him out. He didn't move, but watched them. As soon as she sealed the wound at the second man's neck he climaxed too. Megan was backing away from the two men when the one in the shadows moved toward her.

Megan could smell him. He didn't smell like anyone she'd ever smelled before and that made her nervous. She moved back further as he kept walking toward her. She was nearly to the edge of the light herself when he stepped into the light enough that she could see him.

Christ. He was big and not only big, but he was beautiful. Shaking her head Megan turned and ran from the area. She was nearly three miles away when she realized that she wasn't alone. There were wolves here, big ones too.

Megan sat down next to one of the big trees in the open forest and stilled. She knew that she could sit this way for hours and no one would ever feel her. Twenty minutes later the man, the one in the shadows, walked right by her. The wolves, silent now, didn't move when he did.

Megan waited another ten minutes, sure that he was gone before she rose. Smiling at the wolves she thanked them for their added help and began playing with them. It was nearly ten o'clock at night when she moved away to go to work.

Chapter 2

Kyle paced his office. He wasn't a very patient man and he knew this. He was hoping that his mate, Madison, would hurry up and show. He knew that she could calm him in ways that nothing else could. His friend Beau had better be on time too.

Beau Desjardin was coming for an extended visit. Kyle didn't know why, nor did he particularly care, but he was glad for the visit. He and Beau had been friends for more than two hundred years, since Kyle had been visiting France during the war.

He'd met Beau just after the French war. He'd been wandering around in a slight daze and Kyle had come upon him, thinking to find a quick feed. He didn't care for feeding from men, but he was starved and desperate. It wasn't until he was nearly next to Beau that Kyle realized that Beau was a newly turned vampire.

When Kyle had tried to help the younger man he'd been surprised at his strength. A newly turned vamp was normally weak and very easy to kill. Beau had not only knocked Kyle on his ass a couple of times, but managed it on a massive amount of blood loss and not knowing how to replenish it.

Taking him under his wing Kyle showed him the basics and also showed him how to make sure that he had what he needed to survive. Not just in the human world, but also among the predators like themselves.

Beau had become a master some decades back and had retired with honor among his kind. A rare thing for a vamp to retire; they were normally killed for their position and power. But Beau had managed to not only do that, but also retire with the blessing of the Vampire Council as well.

"Will you please sit down? You're wearing a hole in that carpet and I am *so* not going to wait for that carpet guy to come back."

Kyle turned to Maddie. "I told you I didn't do anything to him. He was in the way when I came up from our lair and he was…startled, that's all."

Maddie looked at him with a raised brow. She could do that as well as Aaron, his friend. He didn't like it on her any more than he did on Aaron.

"You just happened to come from the lower levels at the same time he was making a pass at me? Get real. We both know you'd been waiting in the corner to jump him ever since I told you he thought I had a nice ass."

Kyle could feel the anger surge through him again at the thought of that man, any man, looking at his mate's ass. That was his and his alone. He turned away before she could see his reaction again. Maddie hated it when he got all possessive like he did.

"He was just there. I don't know why he refused to come back and finish the job. All I did was startle the man."

"Yes, I'm sure you did. You'd startle me too with your fangs to your chin and standing there beating on your chest like some sort of he-man routine. Get real, fang boy, you deliberately scared that man and we both know it. Sit down!"

He sat. Not because she had ordered him to, but because he was getting tired. *Yeah*, he told himself, *you believe that and the one about the Easter Bunny and Santa Claus.* He snorted at her then smiled. "Come here, Maddie. I want to nibble on your skin. I want you again. Please?"

She snorted this time. He was sure he'd picked up the habit from her after thinking about it for a second. He started to stand

and bring her to him when there was a knock at the door. After bidding the person to enter Kyle rushed the man standing there. Beau.

The two men embraced tightly. It had been a very long time and neither man had changed much over the years. But their level of friendship had. They had gone from being friends to becoming as close, if not closer, than brothers.

"Do the two of you need a room or should I just leave? It's getting very…manly in here."

Both men turned to Maddie. Kyle was fighting the tears to keep them from falling. He hadn't realized just how much he had missed his friend. He pulled Maddie to him and held her close.

"Beau, this smart ass is my mate. Madison, this is Beau Desjardin. He and I have been good friends since the French Revolution. He and Aaron are friends as well."

"Bonsoir, Maîtresse. Vous êtes beaucoup plus beau que Kyle avait dit. Je suis très heureux de faire votre connaissance." Beau kissed her hand and bowed before her.

Kyle wasn't sure if he was impressed that he'd been able to render Maddie speechless or if he was angry that he had. He bumped the man from his mate and pulled her back into his arms.

"How lovely," she finally said. "What did you just say to me?" Kyle pulled her tighter.

"I wished you good evening and I said that you are far more beautiful than Kyle had said. I am also very happy to make your acquaintance. You are a very beautiful *femme*, mistress."

"Oh well…thanks. I have to go. I know you two have a great deal to catch up on and I have some people who need their asses kicked. I'll see you both later?"

"We should be back around sunrise. You and the baby make sure that you lock all the doors before you go to bed."

Kyle and Maddie had had a little girl about two years ago. She was the spitting image of her mom and Kyle couldn't be happier with them both. He worried about them constantly and wondered once again if he and Kyle should just go back to the house and talk or go to the Blood Moon as planned.

"Will you take him out of here, Beau? If he doesn't give Angel and me some breathing room we may stake him ourselves. Angel's first words were 'go away, Daddy.'"

"They were not. She did say daddy, but not...will you behave? I swear. Let's go, Beau, before I have to beat my mate."

They were out the door with Maddie's laughter still ringing in their ears. Beau, of course, was having a bit of fun at him too. Kyle decided that he'd make her pay and thought about the hundreds of ways to do that. Top on the list was tying her to the bed and having his way with her until she was screaming for release. *Oh yeah*, he thought, he was so going to make her pay.

~~~

Megan was making her way back to her car after her job at the clinic when she saw the young child being loaded into the back of the van. His limp body made her think he was dead a first, but the way the men were handling him made her rethink that. She was sure he had been drugged. She made her way toward them. "Hey there. Whatcha doing? That's a pretty little boy you got yourself there."

The men stopped suddenly and looked at her. She didn't move a step closer, but she could smell the drugs they'd used on the tiny child. Megan wondered where his mother was, but didn't say anything. She also wondered if the men knew what they had.

She realized that they did. And not only did they know, but had purposely drugged the child because of what he was. A wolf, a young pup of a wolf that she knew they were going to bring untold harm to.

"You be on your way, kid. This is no concern of yours. This here...this is something you don't want to get that cute ass of your'n involved in. Biting off more'n you can chew could get you killed."

"That's real nice of you." She stepped closer to the child. "I don't think you guys are the child's family and if you don't mind, I'll see that he gets there. Now."

The men shifted and so did she. She knew there was one more man coming up behind her and the two in front of her. She didn't want to hurt them, but if they pushed her or tried to take off with this pup she was going to stop them.

"Like I said, don't be biting off more than you can chew. This isn't any of your concern and I suggest, nicely like, for you to move on and forget you ever seen anything." When he pulled out his gun and pointed it at her she decided that she was going to have to get rough with them anyway.

Megan turned and started to the right of the two men. When she was just a few feet from the man who was coming up behind her she lunged at him and hit him in the throat with her fist. She knew she was stronger than she'd ever been thanks, she supposed, to the change, but she didn't realize how much. The man's neck snapped and he dropped to the ground. She hated to kill and for that one fleeting second was sorry, then promptly forgot him.

Turning back to the two men now behind her, she lifted her fists and stepped toward them. In actuality she was terrified. Megan didn't kill, it wasn't in her nature. And though she wasn't one now, her years of trying to become a doctor had ingrained something into her that made her hate killing on a higher level than she'd thought possible. She hoped these two would just walk away, but knew that in reality they'd fight her.

"I don't want to have to kill you, but I will. Why don't we just call it a night and I take the young pup with me and we all live to fight another day?"

The first man laughed. She could smell his fear. She was sure that a healthy part of it was her own so she couldn't really blame the man. The second man seemed to be considering his options. She was sure he was going to get him and his partner killed when he grinned at her.

"If we win, which we will, we're going to rape you over and over until there ain't nothing left of that sweet-smelling pussy of yours. Whatcha think of that?"

She made them think she was considering it when she suddenly grinned at them, showing as much of her fangs as she could without opening her mouth like a horse on display. "Okay. Fair enough. But if I win." She moved toward them with dizzying speed and was suddenly in his face. "If I win, I get to drain you both for my dinner."

She could almost see their minds working this out. Sharp teeth, check. Dark outside, check. Snapped the dead guy's neck like a chicken bone, double check. Vampire. When they continued to stand there she leaned closer and licked her lips. "Go," she told them in a low voice and they took off in a flash. She might have laughed if she hadn't felt the sun starting to beat on her. She knew she only had about thirty more minutes before it would be too late to get anywhere safe.

Picking up the tiny little pup she cradled him in her arms and moved to her car. It was the only thing she could do. He was drugged and she didn't want to burst into flames. Crawling into the back of the car and closing the seats up over the trunk then setting the locks, Megan put the wolf in the blanket next to her and settled down. She hoped the little guy wouldn't wake while she was out. She didn't want him to be scared when he did. Her last thought before sleep claimed her was she should have found him some food.

Chapter 3

"We'll find him. Don't worry, Jacob. He couldn't have gotten far. We have everyone looking for your son."

Bradley hoped he was right. He and his pack had been looking since late last night for the three-year-old son of his best man and pack member. Jacob and his mate Sandra had been out on a run with their son on his first night training and someone had hit them with a tranquillizer gun and drugged them both. When they woke a few hours later JC was gone and they had one hell of a headache.

"It's been so long, alpha. He's only a child. What if he was taken? What if…what if they harm him?" Sandra asked on a sob.

Bradley didn't answer. He wasn't even sure he could. He knew that if anything happened to his own children…he didn't want to think about what he would do, what lengths he'd go to in order to get them back. He looked up at the waning sun and shuddered. Night fall again. He nearly pulled out his cell phone to call his brother when it rang in his hand. Putting his hand over his heart to slow it some he answered the call from David.

"We have a problem. I think we…we have a dead man here and JC's scent all over him. Also…also a car. Bradley, you need to come here. I think we have a vampire situation on our hands."

"I'll be right there. Do we need to call Aaron?" He didn't ask his brother what the problem was knowing that if David was nervous then he was afraid of what his answer might be.

"No. Not yet at any rate. Come here first." He gave him the address in one of the worst sections of the city. "Don't bring Jacob or Sandra. I don't think it will go any better if they're here and upset."

Bradley got into his vehicle and gave his driver the address. He knew the street and agreed with David. Winston Street was not known for anything but drugs, prostitution, and drugs—not necessarily in that order. Then he thought of Aaron.

Aaron MacManus; friend, savior, and master vampire. The man had been around for nearly fifteen hundred years and had the largest realm of vampires in the United States, maybe even in the world. He was fair-minded and very well respected, not only by his peers, but by most of the other paranormals around Ohio. Bradley thought with a sardonic grin that it probably helped that he was by and far one of the most powerful beings in this world and was mated to the cousin of the Queen of all Magick.

Bradley knew that he'd be up. Aaron could withstand sun longer and longer as the years went by and Sara, his mate, helped that with her own magic. Bradley also knew that even if the sun would boil him alive, if Bradley needed him, he'd be there. He just hoped that he wouldn't need him in this particular issue. Pulling up near David's car Bradley walked up beside him.

There were several of his pack members milling around. The dead man David had mentioned was still on the cold ground, but covered with a tarp. Bradley didn't concern himself with him. He knew that his brother hadn't brought him there for him. As Bradley got closer to his brother he could see that a couple of his men were injured. And that the car in question had been damaged.

"We believe JC is in that trunk." David indicated the small sports car with a wave of his hand. Bradley noticed that his brother had blood on his arm and a small cut.

"You *believe* that he's in there? If you believe that, then why haven't you made certain? Or do you need me to do this for you?"

David huffed at him. Bradley merely smiled. His brother had only been his enforcer for a short time, not long enough to get rid of his policeman ways and think like an enforcer for the pack. He grinned when David huffed again.

"Okay, smart ass, you do it. Walk over to that car and try to see for yourself." Bradley looked back at the car. "Oh, and while you're over there you might want to tell your mate that you love her 'cause I'm thinking you'll not be around long enough to tell her yourself when you get there. The thing in that trunk will tear you to pieces."

Bradley looked at the car, really looked. That was when he noticed that most of the damage done to the car was on the trunk and that one of the back windows had been shattered. Looking at his men he noticed that while the wounds were many, they had already begun to heal. He looked back at David.

"Tell me. Tell me what you're thinking and stop beating around the bush. If JC is in that trunk I want him out now."

David nodded. "So do I. I can smell him in there. I don't think the vampire in there wants to—"

"Vampire? I thought you said that I didn't need Aaron. Damn it, David, he has to be involved if there are vamps in that trunk."

"I said vampire. And I don't think she is going to hurt him, but she is terrified. Damn it, Bradley, don't you think I want him back as much as you? He is the same age as mine. But she is terrified."

She. David had said she was terrified. Looking at the car, he tried to smell what his brother had. Vampire, yes, and JC. Bradley could also smell her fear, terror, he supposed too. And something more, something that made the hair on the back of his neck stand up. Blood. And lots of it.

He cautiously walked toward the car. He could smell it more now that he was closer and tried to ignore it in order to concentrate on the persons inside. When he was about five feet away he halted and cleared his throat. "My name is Bradley Wolff, the alpha of this territory. I'd like to speak to the person in the trunk and ask you if the pup you have is harmed."

He didn't think she'd answer. He, in fact, counted on it. When he heard JC whimper he leapt to the car and smashed his fist into hard metal. The hand that came out of the small slot just under the lock tore at his thigh and opened a gash. Blood poured from the wound and he jumped back.

"You do that again and I'll hurt the little boy. He's scared and I want you to go away. I told that other idiot that I just wanted them to back the fuck up, but he keeps telling me no."

The voice sounded angry. Well, Bradley thought, so the fuck was he. He started forward again when he heard JC whimper.

"Please, Alpha, I want my mommy. Will you just go away so she can get away? She didn't hurt me, but I gotta pee something serious. Okay?"

Bradley couldn't let her go, he realized. He'd been hurt and his pack knew she'd done it. If he let her go now they'd hunt her down and murder her. If she was innocent, which he was very much sure she was, she'd be just as dead. Taking another step back, he pulled out his cell and called in the big guns. Might as well get this over with he thought with a grimace. "Aaron, I have a problem. I need your help."

~~~

"All right. I can be there in a few minutes. Don't go near the car again, Bradley. I'd hate to have to explain to Airic that you didn't wait for reinforcements to come in and got yourself drained by another woman. I know you said she hurt you and something has to be done, but wait for me." Aaron hung up the phone in the kitchen and looked over at his mate. "I have to go into town. Bradley said he has a she-vamp that has kidnapped one of his young and she hurt him when he'd tried to get the pup free."

Sara looked up from her plate. Aaron loved to watch her eat and now he was going to miss it. He looked longingly at the cheeseburger and fries that were still steaming on the platter before her. When he looked up at her face he could see her disappointment as well. But also her concern and understanding.

"I'll come with you. The girl, do you know anything about her? Any reason why she'd take the young one?" She was covering the plate with plastic wrap as she spoke.

He thought about telling her that he wanted her to stay here, to be safe, but didn't. He knew several things would happen if he did. She'd come anyway, she would kick his ass when they got back, and she would be angry with him for a long night. He just shook his head and put the tea jug in the refrigerator with the other condiments they had gotten out.

"No. Bradley seemed to think she is terrified and he was afraid she'd hurt the pup and/or herself before she came out. He was also afraid if she isn't involved that, no matter how many times he told his pack, she'd be hunted down like an animal and killed because she'd hurt their alpha. Well, not really hurt him, but he'd been hurt and they'd blame her all the same."

"Hurt? Is he all right? Why didn't you tell me that in the first place? Damn it, Aaron, priorities. That should have been the first thing you said."

Aaron tried not to be insulted that his mate would be that upset about another man, but he knew that Sara loved him. And that her concern for Bradley was because he was an old friend of both of theirs. He tried to tell himself that it wasn't jealously that made him want to murder his friend, but his ability to annoy Aaron. "He's fine enough to have called me. Sara, this part of town where she is, it's not—"

"Aaron, if you value that impressive cock of yours, you won't finish that statement. I'm going. You know as well as I do that I'm an immortal and that my magic can help the child if he needs it. I'm going. Now the sooner you get that into your head, the sooner we can get there and the sooner I can get back here and finish my dinner for you."

He rubbed his hand over her huge belly. The baby, his baby and hers, was nestled there and the bigger she grew with this one, the happier he was. When the baby kicked back at him, he felt rather than saw Sara's knowing grin.

"See? He's telling you to buck up too. Come on. I want to come back here so that we can make love again."

Aaron simply leaned down and kissed her belly then her mouth. He knew when to pick his battles and now seemed the perfect time to do so. He felt a small twinge of anger toward the unknown girl and tried to shake it off. Within seconds they were at their destination.

By the time they got there the girl had left the trunk. Aaron watched in awe as three of Bradley's men sat on the ground nursing what appeared to be broken bones and numerous cuts. With a raised brow Aaron walked toward his friend. "Couldn't wait, could you? Is anything serious?" Aaron didn't think so, but couldn't tell. Wolves, like vampires, could heal fast, but pain was pain.

"No. But she's hurt now too. And I did wait. Something must have spooked her and she opened the trunk and tore through us in no time. Luckily for me, I was just coming back from a bathroom break or I might have been hurt again too."

Aaron looked at the men. Yes, he could see that none of them were very badly hurt. Mostly superficial stuff. He turned to ask Bradley where the girl was when he saw the child.

The little wolf was beautiful. His dark brown hair was highlighted with streaks of gold and black. His fur when he shifted would be a dark gray to brown and his eyes, brown now, would be a dark gold. Aaron saw that the child wasn't harmed, but seemed to be having a good time with the adults holding him.

"He's fine. JC said that he didn't know what happened, but the girl, the vamp, didn't hurt him. He said that he woke up with her sleeping beside him and it wasn't until one of us started to pound on the trunk demanding that he be let out that she woke. It was full daylight when David got here and he wondered if she was in her sleep period."

Aaron nodded. He was very sure that was what she'd been doing. He could smell her now, the vampire. She was young. Very young, he thought, too young to be out on her own and much too young to be without her maker. But he knew that she was. He could smell no other vampires in the area.

"Did she say anything? And which way did she go?" Aaron looked at his mate as she spoke. Now that it was determined that the pup was safe Sara would think about the girl.

Aaron wandered away. He was following her scent, the scent that called to him as a master. She was hurt, as Bradley said, but he didn't know how badly. He was at the abandoned warehouse before he knew it. She was there just in the corner and she was crying.

"Come out, child. I need to see your wounds. I'd also like to talk to you about what happened between you and the pup. There isn't anyone going to harm you."

Aaron didn't put much command in his voice; he didn't feel it was necessary. She was too young to fight him and weak too. He simply waited for her to do as he bid.

"I don't think so. I didn't hurt that kid. He was already unconscious when I found him. You just go away and I'll go about my business."

He felt Sara's laughter run through his mind. She knew his thoughts as well as she knew her own and it rankled him that she'd heard his arrogance. He started to say more to the young vamp, anger about to spill from his lips, when Sara stopped him with a whisper through his mind.

"She's already proven that she's stronger than you thought. I wouldn't piss her off any more than I had to if I were you. Go gently, Aaron, love. She's been hurt too."

"And she'll hurt more if she doesn't learn to obey her master." Aaron took a deep breath. *"You know as well as I that*

she is young. Too young. I don't feel her maker anywhere around and that's a danger all by itself."

"Probably. But she doesn't seem to be hurting you right now. I can't...her mind is a jumble of thoughts. Mostly terror. If you could calm her, I could probably get an idea where she is from."

Calm her. His mate could be so helpful at times. Aaron turned back to the girl and crouched down to her level. He was going to smile, but didn't want to make her think she wasn't in trouble for this.

"JC is going to be fine. He said that—"

"Is that the man? He attacked me and I had no choice but to take him. They were going to...if I tell you what happened, will you go away and forget you ever saw me?"

Aaron wanted to know more, but knew that if he told her yes, he'd be lying to them both. He couldn't let her go. He needed to turn her over to her maker and then reprehend him for not keeping better control over his child. He started to tell her that when he saw her move. Aaron backed up when she stood up completely.

"I want you to move so I can leave. I didn't hurt that kid. When I found him and those men they'd already drugged him. I saved him and I think that should count for...what about my home? Who do you think will pay me for the damage to it?"

Aaron swore a long stream of curses before he looked back at the beat up car. "By your home I'm assuming you mean the car over there, correct? You're living in your car with your maker and he's left you here to do what, pray tell?"

"Maker? I don't...you mean Alfred? The person who made me into this monster? I don't...he's dead. I don't know what happened to him other than the fact that he attacked me one night and did this." She pointed to the jagged scar on her neck. "Then he just disappeared. I guess it was a week later when I woke up in that cave with this feeling...I knew he was dead I felt him die and then fell back to sleep."

Aaron ignored her reference to being a monster. If she was made a vampire against her will it was probably a good thing this Alfred was dead. The Council was very strict on turning without permission.

"When did he turn you? And tell me your name. I'm Aaron MacManus, by the way. I'm master of this realm you're in."

She shifted on her feet. Aaron still couldn't see her face, but he could see that she was a young female. The shadows she was in made her seem small, but he had already figured out that she was bigger than he now thought. She'd have to be to plow through those full grown wolves and live.

"My name isn't any of your business. I don't have a clue what you mean by 'master of the realm.' Sounds like you've been smoking some great weed or you are having delusions of grandeur. I'm thinking the latter of the two."

"It means you're supposed to bow down before him and think he's the best thing since sliced bread. You should listen to him. He gets testy when he doesn't get his way."

Aaron turned to his mate. He was about to snap at her when she gave a very small shake of her head. He would play along until he got answers or until he got his way.

"And that doesn't make you sound like you're having 'delusions of grandeur'? Sounds just like that to me," she whispered again.

He turned back to the woman when she laughed. "Yeah, well you sound just like him. I don't need or want a boss. I'm leaving." She stepped into the light and both Aaron's and Sara's breath caught. Christ, she was beautiful.

Chapter 4

Megan looked at the couple before her. The woman was simply the most beautiful thing she'd ever seen. Tall and willowy, she still looked tiny standing next to the man. Her red hair seemed to glow with colors and light. Megan could smell that she was different, just not how.

The man was huge. Scary huge, Megan thought. She found herself starting to step back, but when he lifted his eyebrow at her she took a step forward then another for good measure. She lifted her chin at the challenge she saw in his eyes. His long midnight hair seemed to reflect all the light from the moon back up to it. She felt stupid when he laughed at her.

"Ah, you mean to challenge me as well? Good. I've not had a good fight in awhile and would welcome the chance to take you down a peg or two."

She moved quickly and flipped him to his back and onto the ground before he finished the word. A blade at his throat had him raising his hands in defeat. Or so she thought.

"I'm a vampire of considerable strength and age. If you bring me down..." She was suddenly on her back and him with her own blade at her throat. "Then you'd do well to bring a knife of silver, not stainless steel."

The blade cut into her skin with a bite. She hissed out the pain and glared at the man over her as he ran his thumb over the tiny wound and then licked it clean from his skin. She didn't know why he'd done that what with all the diseases going around, but it wasn't her problem. Moving quickly again she brought her feet up to his back and grabbed him around the neck, wrapping her feet around him. With a hard jerk, he was off her and she was standing several feet away. He lay there looking up at her and she felt like she'd gotten the upper hand. With a low bow without taking her eyes from him, she ran away. Sometimes running away was better than gloating.

She was nearly to her car when she stopped. The men, wolves, were still there and she knew as she watched that she'd have to find another place to stay from now on. They were loading her home onto a large tow truck and taking it away. She nearly cried for what she'd considered her only thing left of her other life. Moving along the outer perimeter of the group, she spotted the little boy and sighed with relief.

He was with what she assumed were his parents. And they looked so happy to have him back. As she watched, the big man and the woman came over to them and shook hands with the man. Aaron, he'd said his name was, and she wondered again what he'd meant by the "master" stuff.

Megan watched for several more minutes and when the man looked directly toward her Megan knew he could see her. Stepping back into the shadows Megan decided that morning would be here soon enough and started to turn away.

"You can go for now, little vampire, but you can't hide from me. I've tasted your blood and you now belong to me. Come to my home and I'll set you up so that you will not have to live on the streets. There are things we should discuss before you are found by someone who won't be as lenient as I."

The man's whispered comment had her shiver and she nearly went to him. But she stopped. There was something...something not quite right about her need to do as he'd said. Deciding that she needed to find out more about this MacManus person and his comments she made her way to the library.

Megan had gone there a lot when she'd first found herself alone and not knowing a damned thing about what she was. Her thirst for blood had nearly made her sick with need those first few days. She had killed a man when she'd finally given in and did what had come natural to her. She'd puked for nearly an hour afterwards and then had to find another victim.

She was a vampire. Alfred had told her that for sure, the only thing he'd told her. Then he'd left her hurting and sore from his bite. When she'd found that he was dead, his ashes all she could find of him, she went to the library to see what she could find.

There was nothing to it really. Most of the stuff that she'd read before about the monster she'd become was in smut books. She'd seen the television shows and hype surrounding it, but it was nothing compared to the real thing. It was neither romantic nor was it cool.

She was scared most of the time and hungry the rest. Her body ached more in those first few weeks than any other time in her life. She had no clue what had happened to her body or what she could expect from it. The few things she'd been able to figure out had been by error. The hearing stuff nearly made her scream, and the smell, being able to smell everything, had her sick to her stomach from the odors that she had enjoyed so much before.

Then there were her fangs. The first time they had dropped she had nearly passed out from the pain. It didn't hurt anymore when they did it, but she had yet to figure out how to control them all the time. The only time she could make them come out to play was when she thought about biting someone.

Nearly to the library she could feel someone in her head again. He was searching, for what she didn't know, nor did she care, but he was there. Ignoring him for the moment, she went to the back of the big building and opened the window she'd unlocked, herself, last fall. She'd been desperate to find a place to sleep when her car had been towed before.

Going to the section on myths and legends, she found what she wanted quickly and took the book back to the big table. She didn't need a light, her sight was that good, but she did like comfort. Pulling one of the big, overstuffed chairs over she sat down and opened the book up.

There were pictures throughout the book. Most of them were drawings, but there were a few photographs. Even to Megan's untrained eye, she could tell that they were fakes. The teeth were too long in most cases and then there were the capes. She thought that bit of fashion would give it away quicker than anything. It was an hour later when she realized that she wasn't going to get any help there. At a little after midnight she left the library the way she'd come in.

She needed to find a place to die. That's what she'd come to think of the deep sleep that she would fall into when the sun rose. It wasn't anything she had any control over and there wasn't a lot she could do once she was there. She'd only been woken from it once and that was when she'd felt Alfred die. And then today, when the wolves had threatened her in the trunk.

Megan came upon the bar just before closing. It was called Blood Moon. She'd been there before, not inside, but like she was now. Hanging around just on the outskirts of the building, but close enough that she could smell everyone there. Depressed, she went to the caves she'd found herself in that first week.

~~~

"You say that she's a beauty? Why did you let her go if you're sure that she is going to hurt someone?" Beau wondered the same thing that Kyle had asked his master.

He remembered his first weeks, the constant hunger, and the terror of not knowing. He'd been lucky in that Kyle had found him. He couldn't imagine a young vampire in this world, this time in the new world, trying to make her way.

"I'm not sure. But I had the feeling that pushing her at that moment would have been the wrong course of action. Her terror was so strong that I could barely get a touch on her mind."

"Yeah, and she kicked his ass twice. I doubt he had it in him to have a go at her a third time," Sara told them with a hardy laugh.

Aaron shrugged. "I let her beat me. How else was I supposed to get a drop of her blood? I will say this for her, she doesn't fight like a new vamp. And her strength is off the charts."

Beau laughed. He couldn't wait to meet this paragon of wonders and smack her silly. They had done nothing but praise this...this female for many hours. She should be with a mate, not running about kidnapping small wolves. Beau shifted in his seat and looked over at the very pregnant female with Aaron.

He had the right of it, Aaron did. Carrying on the next generation of vampires was what a female was for. He looked at Sara's face and shifted again. Somehow he thought she knew where his mind had gone. He felt his skin heat from it. He knew that his way of thinking was old fashioned, but no mate of his— if he ever decided to take one under him—would be wandering about without protection. When Sara reached over and patted his hand he knew that she had been listening to his thoughts.

Kyle had told him that the MacManuses were a strong and powerful couple. Their children were as well. Beau could feel it, their magic. He didn't doubt that Aaron's considerable age and his vampirism had a great deal to do with it. But Sara had her own bit of magic too, he supposed. He'd yet to witness anything that set them apart from others and held most of his judgment until that time.

"Why do you not believe that I'm what you've been told, Beau? You can't be that ancient that you think women should be in the kitchen, barefoot and pregnant. What are you, about a century and a half?"

He looked over at Sara as she spoke. "I'm two centuries, but that has nothing to do with my thinking. I am a man who…how do you say…*protégé ce qui est le sien.*"

"Protects what is his? So, you'll own your mate? Not let her out of your sight?" He nodded. "Good luck with that one, big boy. Women today are going to tear you apart for that. We speak our minds and go about our own way."

"I'm beginning to see that. What does your master think about you 'speaking your mind,' Miss Sara? Does he not put you over his knee? I would. A woman, *my* woman, would know her place or feel the palm of my hand over her bottom."

Sara's laugher both embarrassed him and intrigued him. He couldn't say why the latter did, but the first was because everyone at the table had turned to look at them. He shifted again. He didn't wear uncomfortable well.

"I hope I'm around you when you try that, Beau, I really do. And I hope for her sake that she doesn't let you. At least as a form of punishment."

Beau wasn't going to comment on that bit for any amount of curiosity. Sara was too outspoken for his taste and he mentally added that to his list of attributes his mate would have and not have. She would be as quiet as a mouse unless he gave her permission to speak.

He mentally went over his list. Knowing that his mate would be a beauty would be a given. All women were to him and he doubted that the one he'd spend eternity with would be any less so. He wanted someone quiet. He enjoyed his time in solitude and would require his mate to allow him that time every day. She would be a good mother, raising their children to be what he'd been raised to be. He frowned.

He'd had a strict childhood. He'd seen the servants' children run about outdoors while he and his sister had been made to study and to sit quietly while his parents entertained. His parents believed that children should be seen but never heard. His mate would do no less for their own.

She would also be brilliant. He would want someone he could hold an intelligent conversation with. Beau didn't figure to involve her in the day to day business of his life, but he did want her to be able to add something to the conversation if asked.

Beau looked over at Sara and Aaron. He didn't understand them, or the master. How he could let her be so...opinionated was beyond him. But he was only going to be here for a few more weeks before he had to move on. His businesses kept him moving and he didn't enjoy sitting idle for long anyway.

Chapter 5

Megan needed to get herself somewhere to stay. She had been staying in the caves for three days now and she hated it. She either wanted to get her car back, which she didn't want to risk going for, or an apartment. She was a creature of habit no matter what sort of monster she'd been made into, and she wanted a shower. But to do that she needed more money.

She knew that an apartment would be a major undertaking. It needed to be in the basement somewhere and it needed to have minimal windows. A kitchen would be a waste, but she knew that asking for an apartment without one would raise a few eyebrows. She had tried to eat something that first month and had made herself majorly sick for her effort. She wouldn't be doing that anytime soon.

It was full dark when she got to the bar again. Blood Moon had a reputation for being a vampire and werewolf place to hang out. She'd overheard one of the people who worked in the kitchen say they needed extra help. Megan had tended bar to work her way through most of her college tuition and books. Taking a deep breath she entered the bar from the front door.

The place was huge. The bar itself was at least twenty feet long and a dark cherry that gleamed under the lights overhead. There were stools about every two feet, leaving enough room between them to accommodate standing by it and ordering. Megan could see the long line of liquor behind the bar and looked to have five different set ups. That would mean that on a busy night, there could be as many as five bartenders working the crowd.

The floor was a lighter cherry and reflected back the indirect lighting that was in the ceiling above it. She had never seen a bar so lit up before. No dark corners or blank space here. She supposed that it would help to keep the problems down that came with most bars. Tables were spread all over the room, booths along the outer walls were deep and had a light over each one. There was a stage; large speakers and a microphone was all that was set up at the moment, but Megan thought that it would hold a good-sized band without any problem. She could see the kitchen area from where she stood, but nothing more than a swinging door and a fountain pop machine.

Megan made her way to the bar end closest to the front doors. Of the five people standing there, she knew that one of them had to be in charge. She thought at first glance it was the woman who was wearing a nice suit and looked to be a model, but dismissed her for someone who, while in charge of something, it wasn't the bar. The other two women were dressed like waitresses, their clothes suggestive without being too brazen and their eyes had the look of those who were bored out of their minds. The man who stood against the bar was too...well, he was just not the right type, she supposed, to run a bar of this size. He was too flamboyant and much too unsure of himself to be a boss. The man in the brightly-colored tourist shirt was the one she needed to talk to. He gave off the appearance of being just laid back enough to let you get close enough then he'd rip your throat out when you crossed him. That thought made her stop. He turned to look at her when she did. She didn't move when he stood up and started toward her.

He didn't say anything as they stared at each other. His name tag over his heart said he was the manager, Kyle Dixon. She looked back up at his face and wasn't surprised to see the tip of his fangs as he smiled. Megan looked at the woman, the one in the nice suit who came to stand next to him. She spoke first.

"Hello. Can we help you?"

Megan didn't answer at first. Waves of nausea hit her hard and she staggered slightly. The man started to reach for her, but Megan took a step back and into someone behind her. Before she could turn he grabbed her around the waist and she felt the first grip of terror.

"Let me go." Megan knew it was the man from the other night. She could smell him. She tried to turn, but he simply held her tighter and told her to behave.

"We're not going to hurt you. Your hunger is beating against us and we're trying to keep you from attacking anyone in here. Why the fuck didn't you feed before coming here?"

"I don't attack people. Let me go, you overgrown ox." She brought her foot down hard on his instep and moved out of his arms when he jerked back. "I want to go. I made a mistake coming here. Move."

He stood in front of the door and the man and woman flanked her right and left sides. Megan didn't have to turn to know that there were others behind her. She knew that she couldn't win against those odds.

"Tell me why you came here and I'll think about letting you go. You are in my realm, young lady, and I run the show, not you."

She must have looked confused because he cocked a brow at her. "I'm the master, Aaron MacManus. You are in my realm and, being so, I am your master. You must obey me above—"

"I obey no one, least of all a self-proclaimed master." There was enough scorn in that last word to tell him what she thought of him.

The man behind her, Kyle, laughed, but a quick look from the man in front of her had him turning it into a cough. The woman had no such problems and kept her laughter going until Aaron cleared his throat.

"Oh, Aaron, you know as well as I do that you are as impressed as we are. Not many would stand up to someone of your power or badassness. Let the girl speak and we'll get to the bottom of this. Come on, Miss…"

Megan looked at the woman and realized she was powerful. Not like Aaron, but no less powerful. Megan turned with the woman, but kept an eye on the Master Dingdong or whatever he said he was.

"Megan, Megan Reed. I came…I need a job. But I can only work nights, no daylight at all. I'm…I have a problem with the sun."

Megan didn't know what others knew about her. She could tell when someone was different, most of the time she could even tell if they were vampires or werewolves, but nothing much more than that. Some had a certain scent about them, but it wasn't anything she knew to associate with any one type of paranormal.

"Yes, so does my mate. I'm Madison Dixon, by the way. Come on, let's get you something to eat then we'll talk. You need a job, you say? What can you do?"

"Tend bar, but I don't eat. I don't…I'm not hungry." Not for food at any rate, she thought. "If you could tell me whether or not you have an opening I can be on my way."

Megan walked with the woman. It occurred to her that she seemed to have little to no choice in the matter. Before she knew it she was in an office and the door was closed behind them. They were seated on the big couch and Megan had a glass of blood when Miss Dixion started to talk.

"I've not seen you here before. Tell me about yourself. How did you hear about Blood Moon?"

Megan looked in the glass in her hand and shuddered. It wasn't that she didn't trust the woman who gave it to her—she didn't actually—but it was the fact that she had to drink it to survive. Miss Dixion cleared her throat and had Megan looking up at her.

"I can't offer you my vein. We have people who donate themselves. I'm sorry if you don't like your dinner this way, but I want to talk to you before I let you go on the patrons of the bar."

Miss Dixon knew what she was. Megan didn't know why that didn't surprise her, but it did a little bit. She looked around the office again and realized that she couldn't...shouldn't be here.

"I understand. You don't know me any more than I know you. Yet you expect me to trust you with a glass of this." Megan set the glass on the table in front of her. "I'll get what I have to later. And not here." She stood.

Maddie didn't move. "I can make you tell me, but I'd rather not. I can make you drink that, but again, I'd rather not. Sit down, Megan Reed. We are in the middle of an interview and it's considered bad form to leave before I offer you a job."

There was just enough push in her voice to make Megan sit. She'd read about it, compulsion, the smut books had called it. Megan wondered if she could possibly do it as well and fought against the hold and stood again. She wasn't sure which of them was more surprised. "I'm not your slave either. I'm leaving and I'd like to do so without having to hurt you. It's been very nice to meet you, but I have things—"

The door opened behind her and Megan turned to see who it was. The first man she recognized as Kyle Dixon; the second was the man from the other night, the King Dingdong. The third was an unknown.

~~~

Beau entered the large office behind Aaron. He'd only come here to meet up with Kyle and they were going to go fly together. But the man was so besotted with his mate that he had to go and "let her know so she didn't worry" before they left. The young woman in the office with Maddie startled him.

She was beautiful. She was a classic beauty, long hair, tall and willowy frame. When she turned to glare at Aaron he grinned until she turned her eyes on him. Beau felt as if someone had hit him in the gut. Christ, she had the most beautiful eyes he'd ever seen.

Pewter, a polished pewter, stared back at him. When she turned fully he got a full view of the total picture of the woman. Her hair was long and blond, a white blond like he'd seen small children have in the summer when they'd spent their days out of doors. Her skin was a light golden brown that made him think of the beaches in California and the women who lay in the sun for hours. However, she didn't look leathery like they did, but soft and smooth.

Her nose was small and sloped; brows dark against her skin arched perfectly over those gorgeous eyes and stared unblinkingly back at him. Her lips looked lush and full, kissable, he thought. Like she'd spent the entire night being kissed and begged for more. Before he could finish his assessment of her she started toward him. A slow, sexy gait that had his cock jerk in response. When she was standing inches from him he was surprised when he realized she was a vampire, young but like him.

They stared at one another for several seconds. Then she leaned close and buried her face in his neck and inhaled deeply. Beau groaned at the feeling of her breath on his skin, the heat of her body searing against him. When she started to pull away he instinctively put his arms around her and pulled her back, leaning in to take his own breath of her. Ocean and sunshine, sand and tanning lotion, bodies sliding over one another slick with sweat—these scents and sensations tumbled over his body as he licked her throat, tasting more of her. When she suddenly jerked back it was all Beau could do not to growl at her.

"I have to...I have to get out of here. Now, I have to leave now." Her voice was breathy and soft, but Beau could hear her and he stepped in front of her to stop her from leaving.

"No." He looked at Aaron then at Kyle and knew that they were as aware as he what this female was to him. It made him step back, but not out of her way.

"Beau, is she…is Megan your mate?" Kyle looked at Maddie and before he could deny or agree with her question the woman moved toward the door again.

"I said no," Beau thundered, and struggled to calm his voice. "Sit down, *mademoiselle*. We must talk about what has happened to us."

"Us? I don't think so. The last time someone licked my neck he turned me into a monster. Not again, never again, thanks. I'll be going now and I'd appreciate it if you would just move the hell away from the door."

Aaron moved forward and, with a flick of his wrist, a chair was suddenly behind the female and she was sitting in it. Beau was impressed and a little pissed at the same time. She was his mate and he would handle her.

"I would like a word, if you please? I have to explain to the young…what is your name, *mademoiselle*, so that I can address you properly?"

The girl simply glared at him. Beau wanted not to be impressed with her, but he found it hard to resist her stubbornness. He would deal with her obvious disobedience in a moment. For now he wanted to set down the rules of their relationship. He looked at Maddie with a raised brow.

"Oh no, big boy. You're on your own here. If you get her name, it'll be from her, not me. Sara told me your views on you and your mate." She sat in the big chair again and looked ready to watch. "Go ahead, ask her—no, sorry—demand it again."

"I do not see the humor in this. She is my mate and there needs to be rules. *Merde!* The sooner she learns her place in my life the better things will be for her."

Aaron sat too and the female jumped up from her seat immediately. Beau had only a moment to look at the master before he was defending his body against her fists. She was a wildcat and while he may have appreciated this in a woman, not in his mate. He brought her close to his body to subdue her before she was injured.

41

When her tiny fist connected with his nose and her foot his balls he tried to be calm, but the pain was too much and he grabbed her leg as he fell to the floor. He hung on even as the pain radiated throughout his body. When a pain exploded in his head his last thought was he'd made a mistake. This could not be his mate.

Chapter 6

Megan was furious. The nerve of that man thinking he could just treat her like she was some small child. And rules! She'd show him rules the next time he tried that crap on her. But his smell, the way it had called to…she wasn't going to think of that right now. She had to find another job and find it quick. She thought longingly of her car.

It had been her last touch with her human side. The only thing she'd had left that she could feel beneath her fingers that had been hers. She did have her letters, the one from the Board of Medicine, but it had done her little good after she'd figured out the sun thing. She thought back on those first few weeks and shuddered.

She'd had no idea how much time had passed when she woke in that cave. It had actually been only a week, but she felt as if it had been months. Her body had ached in ways she'd thought she'd had a bad case of the flu. But somehow she knew that it was much more than that. Fear had her stay in the cave throughout the night. Fear of Alfred coming back and fear that he wouldn't. She didn't have any idea where she was and sat watching the opening of the cave for hours.

Toward dawn she realized that she couldn't sit there any longer and moved toward the opening just as the sun was rising. Her body felt tired, beyond tired really, and she thought she'd take a nap first, but wanted to find someone to help her. Alfred had kidnapped her and she wanted to get back home.

By the time she was several yards from the opening, she realized that she was feeling strange; her body and mind felt heavy and she could hardly keep her eyes open. And she hurt.

At first she thought it was her imagination. She'd always tanned easily and couldn't understand why she felt as if she was burning. Her belly began to rebel at the heat and her skin blistered. Megan turned back to the cave just as large blisters formed on her arms. Running now, she made her way back to the cave just as the pain became nearly unbearable. Screaming from a mixture of pain and terror Megan made it inside and fell into a deep sleep as soon as she was in the darkness. She thought at the time that she had died.

She woke that night hungry and still blistered. Cautiously, she made her way out into the darkness and moved toward the lights she could see in the distance. Her belly rumbled and she was hungrier than she'd ever been. But somehow she didn't think she wanted a cheeseburger and fries.

The sounds were so loud that she felt as though she had to cover her ears, and the scents? She could smell everything from the sweat on someone's body to the smell of vomit in the alley. Her head hurt, as did her eyes and belly, and she knew that she had to find relief soon or go insane. When she came upon the man in the alley pissing, she moved up behind him so quickly that, at first, she didn't know what to do. Then her fangs had dropped.

Pain shot through her head and mouth, blood poured from her gums, and she felt as if her mouth was being ripped apart. When she swiped her tongue over her teeth, she cut herself with the sharp incisors. But the explosion of taste in her mouth made her leap at the man before her. She was at his neck with her teeth deep before she even realized what she was doing. Jerking back from him, blood poured from her bite and she nearly left him, but the doctor in her made her grab at his wound to try and stop the bleeding. Hunger tore at her until she'd had no choice in the matter and leaned down and covered it with her mouth.

Rich and hot, it poured into her mouth. Her hunger was so great that she continued to drink greedily long after she should have stopped. When she finally lifted her head, she knew that she'd killed him. Dropping his body from her lap, Megan jumped up and backed away until her back hit the wall behind her. She'd killed a man. It didn't matter that she didn't mean to, or that she had no idea what she'd done. He was dead and she was responsible. She made her way back to the cave and stayed there for four days hoping that she'd either die of starvation or that someone would come along and kill her. Megan had never been so depressed in all her life.

~~~

Sara MacManus was sitting in the living room when Beau came up from the lair. He didn't know how he'd ended up in the master's home, but was grateful that someone had seen to him when he'd been hurt.

Beau refused to think he'd done anything wrong or anything that warranted his mate to treat him like she had. He'd only been looking out for her best interests. He bristled when he thought about how everyone had seen her bring him low. He would have to have a word with his female. Just as soon as he found her that was. Beau was nearly across the room and out when Sara spoke.

"Have a seat, Beau Desjardin. I would like to discuss a few things with you."

"I've things to see to, mistress. And I have need to find Kyle. He and I had plans for this night and—"

"Perhaps you didn't understand. I didn't ask you to come and sit with me, I told you to do so. Now sit."

Beau didn't have a choice. She was as much his master when he was in this realm as Aaron himself. He moved over to one of the couches and sat lazily onto it. Beau looked at the mistress of the realm much like he'd done his female from the night before.

"If she doesn't hit you again, I'll be surprised. You are an arrogant bastard, aren't you? She has a name, use it."

"I'd prefer that you stay out of my thoughts. They are mine and mine alone. As for the female." Beau used the title harshly. "I do not know her name."

"Megan Reed. She isn't going to be a pushover, you know that, right? No, I can see that you don't. I plan to have her here tonight. You, of course, will not be. Here, I mean. I have things I'd like to find out about her and it will go much better if you and your medieval thinking weren't here."

Beau sat up straight and was slammed back against the cushion before he could speak. He tried to break free, but all that did was tighten the bands around his chest and legs.

"What's the meaning of—"

"Shut up. You seem to think that this is all a game. Well, I've got news for you, bucko, you do *not* want to fuck with me. I have more power in my one finger than you could ever hope to wield. When I tell you we're going to talk, then we are going to talk."

His fangs dropped and before he could do much more than take a deep breath to shout at the mistress to let him go he felt the first trickle of fear. Power surged in the room and made it feel as if it had expanded with it. He looked at the woman who stood before him and wondered if he was going to live.

"For now. You'll listen to me because if you don't, then I will go to your own master and demand your head. I'm in no mood to fuck with you over this. What do you know about Megan?"

"She's my mate. I don't need to know any—"

"Don't," Sara snapped at him. "I had the opportunity to search her mind last night. Something you should have done before you started spouting off rules and regulations like a drill sergeant."

Beau shifted in the seat, as much as she would allow anyway. He hadn't done that or anything else. He'd found his

46

mate and he'd taken. Not that he could think how it was any business of this woman's.

"I make it my business."

Beau looked at her. "Would it be easier for you if I just let you rape my mind and not bother with conversation? I cannot see how you are treating me any different than my treatment of the fe…Megan."

Sara sat down. "She was turned against her will. Someone named Alfred took her humanity and made her what she considers a monster. She lived in her car until a week ago and now she lives in a cave." She looked up at Beau with tears in her eyes. "She means to end her life as soon as she figures out how to do it."

Beau struggled against the bonds that held him. He would find her and make… "If what you say is true then how will I keep her from succeeding? She will end it whether I am her mate or not, won't she?"

"Yes. I believe she will. She is clueless as to what she is. I'm not sure how she has survived all this time. I don't know what happened to her maker, but he's dead. Well, at least she thinks he is. Will you listen to me if I allow you to move?"

What he wanted to do was storm out and find his mate, but Sara was right. He did need to know what to do. This was not turning out the way he'd thought it would. When Sara laughed, he looked up at her. "I will stay, but I would prefer that we speak our minds, not listen in. It's very…uncomfortable when you know all my thoughts."

"Very well. But don't give me a reason to listen again. Every vampire in Aaron's realm is precious to us. We'll not have one harmed through stupid thoughtless deeds."

Beau didn't say anything, but took a deep breath as soon as she let him. He didn't want to admit it, but she had been right. He would lose his mate if he didn't listen to this woman. He'd already formed a bond with Megan and wanted to go and find her and keep her safe. "Do you know where she is now? You said she was in a cave, do you know where that might be?"

"I don't, but Aaron does. He's speaking with the wolf pack now to have them protect her. The alpha, Bradley, is a very good friend of ours and if anyone can see to her safety, he can."

Beau stood, but before he started to pace, as was his habit, he looked to Sara. At her nod he walked over to the fireplace and then back twice before he felt calm enough to speak. "I would bring her here for me to protect. She is my responsibility, not that of the pack. And before you yell at me again, I will tell you that I was incorrect in my first dealings with her."

"No matter how you dress it up, she's still going to know you're admitting you were wrong. Hello, Beau. Welcome to our home." Aaron MacManus stood in the doorway as he spoke.

He was an impressive vampire. Even if Beau didn't know he was a master he would guess it. Looking back at Sara as she stared at her mate Beau could see the love and respect that they had for one another. He wanted that he suddenly realized. All the things he'd said about his mate were things he'd heard from his own father. Beau sat down.

His father had treated his mother like a thing rather than a person. She'd had no answers for him when he'd lived with them, as had none of the women of his family. They would send him to his father or a male elder when he wasn't around. Even his sisters were subject to the same treatment and had probably been treated that way by their own husbands.

"She will never trust me. That is why you don't let me go to her." It was humiliating and humbling to know that his mate needed to be protected from him.

"Not just you. Her mind is a jumble of misinformation. She has no idea what she is. To her, she is a monster. What little knowledge she has about herself is half truths and myths. She believes that she can starve herself to death and is currently working toward that end as we speak."

Beau stood. He couldn't, wouldn't, let her end her life that way. Not while he could do something to prevent it. He paced and thought aloud. "I must go to her and speak with her. She and I, we need to bond and mate so that I can know where she is.

How do I do that if she won't let me near her?" Two more trips across the room and back. "Woo her. I will *curiam suam* and make her see that I am not a *barbarus*, a barbarian."

"Courting her could work. You know how to do that, I assume?" Aaron had a look that Beau didn't like, but he didn't comment. Sara had a look too, but he knew what that could mean.

"*Oui*, I am French, we invented the courting process. I will begin tonight. I will…you will bring her here, yes?"

"Yes. She will come to me. She won't like it, but she'll have to come." Aaron stood and put his hands on Beau's shoulders. "You fuck this up and I will let Sara have her fun. She's in the last months of her pregnancy and she would like nothing better than to beat the living shit out of you right now."

Beau looked over at the beautiful woman who looked as though she wouldn't hurt a fly. He knew that looks were deceiving and shuddered to think what "beating the living shit" out of someone meant.

"I will not fuck this up, sire. This I promise."

Chapter 7

Megan was on her way back to the cave when she noticed the wolf. He'd probably been following her for some time, but she'd been so wrapped up in her thoughts that she'd missed him. When she stopped, so did he.

"Go away. Shoo. Go back to your home or den or whatever. I don't want to play tonight."

He sat down on his butt and cocked his head at her. Then something occurred to her. She could piss him off. "If I attack you will you defend yourself against me, little wolfie? I think if you bite my neck really hard with your big teeth, you could take off my head." She picked up a stick and swung it at him. "Come on, come at me."

He backed up when she swiped at him. "Damn it. You can't be afraid of a stick, can you? Come on, attack me."

"He won't. Not if he wants to live through the next hour. Hello, my dear, I've come to take you to my home."

Megan whirled around, pulled the stick up, and pointed it at the man behind her. She didn't know this man. But he looked familiar. Taking several steps back she nearly stumbled over the log behind her. "I'm not going anywhere with you. I don't know you. Now leave me." She heard the wolf growl and wondered if they were together. "You've been following me. The man from the other day, you were there when I fed."

"Yes. I'm not going to hurt you, but you are mine. When you killed my child you became my property and I have come to collect. Come with me and I'll cause you no more harm than necessary."

Megan wanted to die, but not like this. This man meant to cause her pain and a great deal of it. She didn't think he'd stop if she told him to either. "No thanks. I don't know who your kid is, but I'm sorry if he's dead. I didn't know how to stop once I started drinking and I killed that man. Sorry, but that's all I know."

He took a step toward her then another. There was a slight breeze that brushed over her face, then heat. Suddenly, there was a man standing in front of her, his back to her. As soon as he spoke she knew real terror. Aaron MacManus.

"You're in my territory without permission. Who are you and what do you want of this child of mine?" His voice was razor sharp, like a blade cutting through silk. He wasn't talking loud, but even Megan could feel the bite of his anger.

"I claim her in the name of the Vampire Law. She killed my child and I want my boon. Even the great Aaron Xavier MacManus cannot condemn another master for that."

Megan stepped around Aaron. His growl had her turn to glance at him. "I told him I was sorry. I didn't mean to kill that man. But I didn't know how to stop and he died. If he makes it quick, I'll let him kill me and he'll be satisfied and there won't have to be any more bloodshed over this."

Aaron shoved her behind him again and Megan hit the ground. She nearly stood up, but was knocked back again. Her head exploded in pain. When she started to stand again something snapped at her arm and held it. The wolf had her forearm in his mouth and while he didn't break the skin, he could very easily.

The night was very bright, the moon shone over the two men fighting in an eerie kind of light. They were fast and violent in their movements and before long it was over. At least she thought it was. One man stood still and looked to the sky. When he turned toward her the wolf let her go and backed away. Megan scrambled back quickly to get away as well.

"When I put you behind me, stay there. What the fuck were you going to do, get yourself hurt more? Damn it, woman. Sara is going to be pissed as it is and if you're hurt…are you hurt?"

"Don't you yell at me, you overgrown asshole. I had it under control. You just had to be this big vamp and step in where you didn't have any right to." Megan stood up and punched Aaron in the chest with her finger. "What the fuck do you want anyway?"

"This is the gratitude I get for saving your ass? You have any idea what he had planned for your hide? You ungrateful twit. I hope that Beau brings you over his knee for your stupidity."

Megan turned away then back around. Her fist connected with Aaron's nose so fast he had no time to dodge it. When he hit the ground, not from the impact, but from complete surprise, she stood over him.

"I don't care what he had planned for me, don't you understand? I'm a monster, I killed his child. Don't you know what that means? All those years of training and for what? I become a murderer and a monster all in one night."

She turned away to leave. Tears of frustration blinded her for a moment or she would have seen the man before her. When she ran into his chest the smell of him hit her system quickly and had her leaning into him again.

He smelled of apples and cinnamon. She had no idea a man could smell like that, but he did. Warm and soft came to mind, though again he was far from it. His body was hard and tight. His muscles moved under her hand and cheek like a well-tuned machine. She pulled back quickly, but not quick enough to get away from his arms tightening around her.

"No, please do not leave. I enjoy you there, Megan. Come, let me make you mine. We will settle the other differences later."

She shoved him. Megan didn't mean to hurt him again; she just had had enough of these idiots telling her what she was going to do. When he stumbled over the wolf just behind them she nearly burst out laughing when the wolf yelped and the man cursed. He was very good a stringing them together very colorfully. The wolf shifted and stood up.

"Christ, you're naked." Megan turned her back to him quickly and now faced Aaron. He didn't look any happier than the man behind her.

"Megan Reed, I've had more than enough of your antics tonight. You'll come back to the mansion with me and we will finish this once and for all." Aaron's voice thundered over her.

"Fuck you, King Dingdong. That bare-assed man behind me took my car; the one on the ground, the asshole that thinks he can set down rules and regulations like my fucking daddy, is making me want to murder him, and you? You walk around like some sort of lord of the assholes and tell me you are my master? I don't think so. I've had it up to my eyeballs in arrogant, demanding men. I'm going home."

Megan would wonder for days how it happened. One second she was stalking off toward the cave and the next she was in a house. She jerked her arm from the lord of demands and backed away from him. When arms came about her waist to stop her she looked over her shoulder to see the Master Dingdong standing behind her. She looked around for the wolf and was happy to see he'd not made the trip with them.

"He can't teleport. But I'm sure he'll be by later to see how things are. For some reason Bradley thinks very highly of you," Aaron told her softly.

"Come here, Megan, and have a seat. These two will leave us alone and we'll have a nice conversation. Aaron, take Beau for a little walk, please?"

Megan looked at the very beautiful woman sitting on the couch. She looked ready to pop she was so far along in her pregnancy. Suddenly, Megan was dizzy and sat down hard on the chair closest to her. The man the woman on the couch had called Beau was pressing her head between her knees.

~~~

Beau could feel her hunger and wondered why she didn't say something. When he looked over at Sara, he knew without a doubt that Megan meant to die by starvation just as she had told him. He'd never seen a vamp die that way, but he knew from stories that it was a long and painful process. When Sara and Aaron sat down together Beau lifted Megan's chin with his finger.

"I've treated you badly, *ma très chère*. I am sorry. Come, you must feed. I will offer you my vein and you will take what you need." The tears in her eyes nearly had him gather her into his arms, but at this point he wasn't sure she wouldn't try to hurt him again. He simply ran his thumb over her cheek and smiled.

"Let me go, please? I don't want to be here. I just want to be left alone. I murdered that man's kid. Don't you see what that means?"

Before Beau could answer her, Aaron spoke up. "You didn't murder his kid, Megan. You couldn't have. If you had tried, another vampire would have killed you. While you are very powerful, I can't believe that you'd kill another of your kind."

"A vampire? I didn't…the only person I've killed was a man. He was just there when I found him. He was taking a leak in the alley and I drained him dry. He was dead before I left. But he wasn't any vampire."

She sat up when Duncan, the houseman to the MacManuses, walked into the room with a tray. It was the biggest thing she'd ever seen and it was filled with all sorts of pastries and two empty glasses. When he set the tray on a small table she noticed a bag of blood. Her fangs dropped so quickly that she covered her mouth to hide them. Beau reached over and moved her hand away gently.

"I've brought refreshments for the missus. And Master Bradley said that the young miss would need nourishment as well. I hope you do not mind, Master Beau, but I thought you could serve her." Duncan handed Beau the glass. "Master, there is a matter of the alpha in the kitchen. He would like to know...that is to say, he needs something more...protective upon his body, if you please. He said to tell you that whatever you have as long as it is not leather. He said that it chaffs his skin terribly."

Aaron laughed long and loud. Beau grinned. Duncan looked confused. When Megan stood Beau pushed her back into the chair and got up to fill a glass for her. He would have rather she drank from him, but soon he told himself.

"Are all men in this family like this?" Megan looked over at Sara and asked. "I mean so pushy that you want to slug them on a minute-to-minute basis?"

"Yes. Yes, I'm afraid they are. They think they mean well, but they only make matters worse." Sara grinned at Megan when she took the glass. "But they do come in handy on occasion. About this man you killed. How sure are you that he wasn't a vampire, Megan?"

Blushing brightly, Megan looked over at him. Beau wasn't sure what she was thinking, but was intrigued by the pink in her cheeks. When she drained the glass and handed it to him he refilled it without thought.

"He had a...he enjoyed...he enjoyed himself when I bit him. I only just figured out that, you know, men enjoy it when I take from them." Her blush brightened and she smiled. Then Beau realized what she was saying.

"You won't be feeding from men again, *mon amour*. That is something else I need to..." A clearing throat from Sara had him stop and rethink his words. "Something else that I would like to discuss with you." Megan glared at him. Somehow, he was sure that he was going to see that a great deal from her over their lives together. He grinned at her and tried to charm her. He was a Frenchman and he knew the art of seduction better than anyone. "Ah, my heart, you wound me with your anger. We are to become mates soon and it would do us well to be friendly, *vous ne pensez pas*?"

She didn't answer, but looked over at Aaron when he walked back into the room with the alpha. "Why don't you think I killed his son? Wouldn't he know that it was his kid? I would think I would."

"He said his child and that you belonged to him through the Vampire Council, the law governing all vampires. The only way he could claim you is through you killing one of his own. If, as you say, the only person you've killed is a human, which by the way, I'm thoroughly impressed that it's only one, then he is mistaken."

"Me too," Bradley said as he took a beer from Duncan. "I don't know a lot of newbies, but you are the most controlled one I've ever meet. Aren't you guys like on a feeding frenzy when you first are made?"

Before he could think of the consequences Beau stood up and picked Megan up. He put her onto his lap as he sat in the chair again. She squeaked and started to struggle, but he simply pulled her to his neck and held her there. As soon as her breath moved over his skin again, he felt his cock harden. She stopped moving and looked up at him.

"Most are. And you're right, she does have control." Aaron moved to the other chair and sat. "Why is that, I wonder?"

Beau thought Aaron was the definition of controlled. He knew the man could get pissed. Kyle had told him that even when he did the man had a will of iron and a head for strategy. "Do not move," he whispered in her ear. "I want you right now, *ma douce*. And we are neither in a place where I can show you how much. Listen to the master and the sooner we get this finished, the sooner we can…talk."

"Megan? Did you hear me?" Beau looked at Aaron and knew that the man had heard him because of the smile on his face. "I asked if you had any other contact with another vampire that may have died at your hand without you knowing."

"No." She shifted in his lap and Beau groaned. "I don't know what he's talking about. I know that—Alfred. Alfred Deveron is dead. He's the guy that…he bit me and turned me into this thing. I didn't kill him, but I know he's dead."

"But you didn't kill him, correct? No, you wouldn't." Aaron stood up and pulled Sara into his arms. "We must retire soon. My lovely mate is tired and I have a wish to see her in her slumber. After I relax her with a bout of lovemaking. You two have a good night."

"Yeah, I gotta get going too. Thanks for the clothes, big guy. I'll have someone bring them back to you in a couple of days. Also, I should bring something over for 'just in case.' Night all." And Bradley left the room ahead of Aaron and Sara.

When the door closed behind the couple too, Beau looked at Megan. To say she looked panicky would have been an understatement.

"You can't have sex with me. Can you?"

Chapter 8

Megan didn't know a lot about men. And even less about vampire men. But she was pretty sure they couldn't have sex. Or so she had thought. The hard cock beneath her bottom lead her to believe that she may have been wrong about that part.

"I can and will have sex with you if you would allow it. Why did you think that I could not?"

She looked away. She was a grown woman with a medical degree, yet talking about her own personal sex life had always been somewhat of an embarrassment to her. She could lecture about sex and the process to others for hours, but her own was a major disappointment.

"I didn't think that vampires could, you know, get hard. I mean, you are, but can you, you know, perform?" She felt her face heat up.

"Why would you think that I couldn't get hard? And, love, look at me, please. I would like to see your eyes when we talk of sex."

She didn't want to, but he'd asked her so nicely that she couldn't help it. She knew that her eyes had turned that hated red. She could see the haze surrounding what she saw and her fangs had dropped, which she didn't understand either phenomenon. But when she looked at him she could see that his had turned as well. Before she could think of her actions she reached out and ran her finger over his lips to see his fangs.

"Mine just come out without any thought to where I'm at or what I'm doing. Can you control yours?"

He nipped at her fingers before he answered her. "Yes. You can as well with practice. Have you ever kissed anyone since you have changed, love?" His voice was low and deep and sent a shiver of something up her spine. Her nipples peaked beneath her shirt and she shifted again on his lap.

"No. I was afraid I'd hurt someone. Not that the opportunity came up, but does it? Hurt, I mean?"

Beau leaned forward as he cupped the back of her head and drew her toward him. She was nervous and excited at the same time. His cock seemed to expand beneath her and she moaned when he pulled her lower lip into his mouth and suckled. Her pussy seemed to swell with her need for this man.

"No. Not if done properly." He moved his mouth along her jaw and toward her neck. "I want to sip from you, taste all of you."

When his mouth skimmed along her neck, she couldn't help but stiffen. He didn't say anything, but moved down along her throat to her shoulder.

"Did he hurt you when he turned you? Did his bite cause you pain?"

Her blood was roaring in her ears and hearing him speak in that low, sexy voice was not helping. She nodded her head and realized that she wasn't answering him. "He kept telling me he was hungry and that he...please, that feels very good. That he was sorry." His mouth was at her ear now and his teeth nipped gently at her lobes.

When his mouth was over hers again she couldn't think, she could only feel. Megan felt him turn her, adjust her somehow, but she couldn't think past what he was doing to her. When he sat back she was sitting astride his lap, her legs on either side of his thighs.

"Unbutton your blouse, *mon cœur. S'il vous plaît*? I wish to see the bounty that is mine."

Megan thought she should be mad about him calling her his, but she only wanted more of what he was doing to her. Her fingers felt clumsy and she couldn't work the buttons correctly, but she finally managed to get most of them undone when Beau simply ripped it open from hem to collar. The sound of the material tearing away made her moan deep in her throat.

"Lift them. Feed me your breasts, Megan. I want you to feed me your luscious breasts so that I may taste your nipples."

Megan cupped her breasts and was amazed at the weight of them. They felt heavier, fuller to her. When her finger brushed against her swollen nipple she groaned and moved her finger over it again and again.

"*Oui*, that's it, make them beg for me, for my mouth." His hands cupped her ass and brought her forward. "Megan, you are so lovely, your nipples are so pink and hard."

He leaned in and licked her, a swirl of his tongue over and over until she was dizzy with need. The heat of his mouth over the tight bud made her grab his head. Tangling her fingers into his hair Megan held him there as he ravaged her, his hands pulling her over his cock until she was riding him up and down.

"I must have you. Please, I need to bury myself deep within you. Tell me that's what you want as well? Tell me you need my cock inside of you, Megan."

She didn't know how she might have answered because he slipped his hands down the back of her pants and pulled them from her body, ripping them open in much the way he had her shirt. Lifting her up, Megan wrapped her legs around him as he moved them across the room. When he pressed her against the wall she moaned again. He was driving her crazy with need.

Suddenly she was lying down, a soft blanket at her back. She didn't know how they had gotten there and, before she could ask, Beau stood, pulled his shirt off, and tossed it across the room.

Christ, he was magnificent. Smooth skin pulled taut over muscles. His dark nipples were peaked hard and Megan found her mouth wet at the thought of taking one of them into her mouth and suckling it in much the same way he had hers. Sitting up on her elbows she watched him open the fly of his pants and slowly move the zipper down along its teeth. She watched him until he stopped and hooked his thumbs into the waistband of them.

"Don't stop, please?" Megan sat up as she begged him to continue. "I want to see you naked. I want to touch you the way you touched me."

"Take off your panties for me. I would see you bare too."

Lying onto her back Megan took off her panties and then what was left of her pants. They hung in tatters from her fingers until she tossed them in the direction Beau had his shirt. Next came her socks and shoes, both flying across the room without a thought to where they landed. When she lay before him naked she looked up at him.

"You. Take them off. I want to see you now." Megan watched as he did as she asked.

Sliding the denim down over his hips she couldn't drag her eyes away from what he was showing her. Lean abs above the waistband of the pants, dark hair, and hipbones muscled with his skin smooth over them. When he pulled his pants lower she could see his cock as it emerged. The dark head and long shaft seemed to leap from his body, thick and hard. She sat up to run her fingers along him. Beau stood perfectly still while she explored him, his pants forgotten at this thighs.

He was harder than she expected, yet smooth at her touch. She watched mesmerized as a drop of cream-colored cum gathered on the tip and before she could think about what she was doing, Megan leaned forward and licked. His moan had her looking up at him.

"*Ne vous arrêtez pas, mon amour. S'il vous plaît, prends-moi dans votre bouche.*" Megan had never been so happy she'd taken French for three semesters in her entire life. She did just as he'd asked. She didn't stop and she took him into her mouth.

~~~

Beau felt his eyes roll to the back of his head as Megan wrapped her mouth around his cock. He wanted to bury himself deep inside of her, but could no more pull away from her now even if the sun was beating down on his head. Wrapping his hand into her hair he gently guided her on how to please him even as he wanted to take her hard and fast.

Looking down at her and what she was doing Beau watched as his cock moved in and out of her mouth, her cheeks hollow and then full with him inside. He was large, he knew, but what she couldn't take inside her small hand covered the rest. Up and down, in and out, he knew at this rate he wouldn't last much longer. Feeling her hand slide up his thigh and cup his balls Beau surged forward. His need to fuck her like this overpowered all reason as he pumped into her wet mouth. When she moaned he felt it race along his cock and curl around his balls. Wrapping his fingers into her hair he pulled her back and, with a soft pop, his cock was free of the most incredible erotic place he'd ever been. He knew her pussy would be better.

"Lay back, love. I will not be able to be gentle this time. I regret that I will not be able to savor as I wish, but you have put me into a state of animal lust to have you."

Before she could answer Beau pulled his pants off with dizzying speed and then waited for her to lay back. She was magnificent.

Her breasts were full and rounded; her nipples were a dusty rose color that made him think of ripe berries. Her waist was small, so small that he was sure he could span it with his hands and touch them together. Hips flared out and framed her pretty pussy.

Megan's tight curls beckoned him; they were wet with her need, her thighs covered in her cream. As much as he wanted to pound into her he needed to taste, to drink from her nectar. Dropping to his knees before her he opened her legs wider so that he could settle between them.

"Beau?" Not wanting her to tell him she didn't want him this way he leaned forward and licked her from gate to clitoris.

She tasted of ambrosia, sweet honey, and cream; warm and spicy to his tongue. Sliding his fingers into her depths Beau suckled her clit into his mouth and laved it with his tongue. He was rewarded with more of her. Liquid poured from her and over his fingers, his hand soaked with her juices. Fucking her with his tongue and fingers Beau felt her tighten around him, her climax imminent. He needed that, her taste as she came. Inserting another then another finger into her, stretching her for his cock, he pressed the little finger of his free hand over the little rosebud of her ass. She surged up off the bed, her climax screaming from her throat.

Still covered in her juices, hot from her pussy, Beau stood. He could wait no longer to be inside of her. Crawling up her body and between her thighs Beau entered her hard and fast. Her body tight, gripped him, strangled his cock. Moving slowly he pulled out to the tip then rocked into her again, hardly noticing when her nails dug into his arms, drawing blood.

"Bite me. Take from my heart. Please, *mon amour*, now."

She licked the pounding skin over his heart, his cock filled with his cum. When she licked the second time, then a third, he growled deep in his throat. Before he could demand that she finish him she sank her teeth deep into his chest. His climax roared through his body and poured into hers. Grabbing her wrist Beau bit her too, bringing her blood pounding at her vein into his mouth and bringing her body to another climax.

Wave after wave of his climax rolled through him. Twice then a third time he came. Never had he been able to perform like this. His body seemed to have a mind of its own until, finally, he could do nothing more than drop onto Megan, his body depleted of all energy. Thankfully, at the last moment he was able to roll to his side, pulling her with him. His last thought before exhausted sleep took him was that they were truly mated and bonded.

Chapter 9

Megan woke sometime after one in the morning. It took her several terror-filled seconds to realize the body next to hers wasn't anyone she had hurt. Then a few more tense seconds to remember where she was. Not that she knew actually, only that Beau had brought her here. Moving carefully, she got up from the bed. Knowing that looking for her clothes was futile she went to the open suitcase sitting on a chest at the foot of the bed. She pulled out the first shirt-looking thing she could find and pulled it on. She was finishing the last button as she opened the door.

She was in a sublevel somewhere. There were small lights along a corridor that lined the long hallway. She noticed that there were several other doors as she went; all of them had a key pad outside of them. She wondered if that was there to keep people in or out, but dismissed it as none of her business. Moving toward the stairs she was amazed at how lovely everything was.

Megan emerged in a dark room with a door. She could see light just under it and could hear voices. Knocking because she didn't have a clue where she was, she opened the door to a kitchen.

"Well fuck me, this can't be good," Megan said softly. There at the table sat the Master Dingdong and Mrs. MacManus.

The little man from earlier was there, as well as a human woman.

"It's nice to see you too," Dingdong said with a smile. "Have a seat. Does Beau know you left him?"

She didn't sit. "Why should he care? I have to go to work. Can you tell me how I get back to where I was? I need to change first."

Dingdong looked at the woman and then back at her. Megan wasn't sure she liked that look and moved toward the door. She knew that she was going to need to make her escape as best she could. He stopped her when he spoke.

"I've finally figured out why I can't control you, Megan Reed. You don't believe that I'm anything more than...what is it you call me?"

Shrugging, she answered, "Master Dingdong. I don't listen to you because you *aren't* going to control me, not that I don't allow you to. I would like to leave. So unless you have some other tidbits of wisdom you'd like to impart, I'm leaving."

"The man who is following you won't stop. He feels that you have taken something from him and he means to get his payment. You will be killed if he decides that is what he wants. If you aren't where Beau or I can protect—"

Megan turned to Aaron, cutting him off. "So what? I offered to die for him. Why should that be any concern of either of you? Back the fuck off. I live *and* die by my own choice." She opened the door and went out. She wanted to slam it, but didn't want to break the glass. It would be just like the Dingdong to make her pay for that too. She moved down the drive and toward the gate. She kept moving at her fast pace and didn't even break stride when she leapt over it without a thought to what she was doing. Megan was nearly a mile from the gate when she stopped and looked back. It was just one more thing she wasn't going to think about. Not today and just maybe not ever.

Master MacManus was going to drive her insane, she knew It. He seemed to think that she belonged to him in a way that scared her. For a few minutes back there she actually found herself wanting…no, needing, to do just what he'd said. In one of the many books she'd read on vampires she'd come across the word compulsion. Now she wondered if that was more fact than fiction. Before she knew it she was at the cave.

She had a few clothes. She was grateful that there were a few stores open on her schedule. She had gotten some things, most of them actually, from her apartment before they had kicked her out for nonpayment of rent. She leaned down and looked at the photo album that had been one of the things she'd gotten on her first trip there.

Megan hadn't opened it yet. She didn't know if she ever would. Her family must miss her; she certainly missed them. She had gone to see them the first few nights after she'd finally figured out what she was. Even then she didn't tell them. She simply told them that she was going away for awhile, that she needed a long rest after so much school. They believed her, had even given her some money to take with her. "An early graduation gift," her daddy had told her. That, too, still lay near the album.

Pulling on a pair of jeans and a shirt and shoes she left Beau's shirt in the cave and made her way to her job. It wasn't a great job, but she got to be in a hospital even if it wasn't being a doctor. Her hours were from three in the morning until five-thirty. When she got there a little before two Thomas let her start to work.

Thomas Reilly was a vampire. He was a nice man and he seemed to love what he was doing. But he was overworked and as far as she knew, was doing an excellent job of putting wolves and other creatures together. All Megan got to do was clean up after each surgery. He was sitting in one of the high-back swivel chairs when Megan went in a room to mop up. She nearly turned and left, but he motioned her to come in.

"I'm about done here. Come in and talk to me a minute or two while you clean up." He turned in the chair and looked at her. "You gonna ever tell me your real name?"

When she had come by to apply for the job she'd told the office that her name was "Jane Doe." No one had said anything and had even hired her. Well, after she'd made a pest of herself over the next several weeks.

She shrugged. "Nope. It wasn't important when you hired me, it's not now either." She squeezed out the water from the mop and set it near the counter. "Besides, why do you care? I'm doing a good job, aren't I?"

"Yes. Yes, you are. But I can't help but think you might be a little over qualified for this job. You smell different tonight. Something you wanna tell me?"

"Nope." After she got all the towels and other paraphernalia cleaned up she moved the bed and the equipment to one side and began to sweep up. After that she dipped the mop in the bucket and after getting it good and saturated, she began to mop.

"I thought so. I have a case I'm having problems with. I'm going to bounce the situation off you. You can just listen. I do better when I can do that. I have a woman whose hubby, for lack of a better term, is trying to impregnate her. He's not having any luck, mind you, but he keeps trying. I'm thinking he's shooting blanks. Can't be sure about that because he won't come in for testing. I've thought about having her bring in a sample, but that…well, that just sounds deceitful to me."

Megan answered before she thought. "He needs to have no sex and wait for her to become fertile. It'll build up a more viable spermatozoon count." As soon as the words left her mouth she knew she'd been trapped. Dropping the mop she turned to look at the doctor. He didn't laugh at her, nor did he crack a smile. He just stared at her.

"I thought you were a nurse. But you're a doctor." Thomas crossed his arms over his chest. "I had my suspicions that first week when you told the nurse that she needed to gather blood gases for that heart attack patient. Then two days ago you helped a nurse out when she was trying to remember the type of surgery that had been performed on her brother. Thoracotomy isn't a common word, nor is it a common procedure you heard here, especially when weres and vamps don't get any disease that would cause the removal of a cancer to the lung."

Megan looked at the door and then back to the man. She was torn. Leave and not have a job or stay and maybe have to explain herself? She didn't know which was worse.

"You can run, but not hide. I can smell a male on you. You've recently met your mate if I'm not mistaken. Aaron MacManus either knows that you're in his realm or he will soon enough."

"He knows me. And I don't have a mate. It was just sex." Megan put the mop back in the bucket. "What are you going to do?"

Thomas looked at her. She wasn't one to fidget, but he made her nervous. She wanted to cry, but after nearly a year and a half of this life she knew it would do her little to no good to indulge in tears.

"What's your name? And are you a doctor?" His voice was gentle, something that surprised her into answering truthfully.

"Megan Reed. I...I was waiting for my results just before I was murdered. I passed my exams twenty-four days after this happened."

Thomas nodded. "And that would be how long? Not much, I'm thinking. And you weren't murdered, young lady. Your life changed, but you aren't dead."

"You think your way, I'll think mine. January, a year ago. I was just getting off work when he took me. And you didn't answer my question. What are you going to do now?"

He regarded her for several more seconds before he spoke. "Nothing. For now. But you aren't going to be working here any longer. Not as a janitor anyway. Starting as soon as you give me your board certification results I'll put you on staff." He stood. "Aaron will have to know, of course. So will your mate."

"I don't have a mate and why does Dingdong need to know?"

Thomas burst out laughing. "I bet that goes over great with him. Dingdong, yeah, I just bet it does. He has to know because

I'm his subject and so are you. Nothing goes on in his realm that he doesn't know about, isn't told about, or hell is paid to whoever crosses him."

He started out the door before she spoke again. "What if I don't want to be a doctor?"

He turned back. "You already are."

~~~

Beau came above stairs in a foul mood. He had awakened and Megan was gone. And not only was she gone, but she was blocking him. Beau wasn't even aware that you could do that as mates. When he saw Aaron and Sara in the kitchen with their children he nearly turned back around again.

"Hello, Beau. Come in and meet my children." Aaron stood and closed the door to the sublevels before he could bolt. "This is my daughter Lizzy and her twin brother Mac. Guys, say hello to Beau Desjardin. Sit down, Beau. We were just discussing the finer parts of being a vampire."

He knew he had little choice in the matter so he sat. The little girl, Lizzy, smiled at him. He could feel her touching his mind and nearly closed her off, but then Mac said something to him and he let her go. Some things up there might not be suitable for a kid, but he didn't invite and saw no reason to sensor her findings.

"Do you like being a vampire, Mr. Desjardin? I'm not a pureblood like some, but I'm immortal like my mom."

"It's Beau and it's all right, I guess. You have a certain…power about you, don't you?" Beau closed his eyes and reached into the child. "Necromancer. I've only met one other like you. She's not such a nice person so I tend to avoid her."

"Yeah, Patrice Skidmore. She's dead. She was my tutor for a little while. Until my daddy broke her neck and my grandda cut off her head for shooting my grandma. Aunt Bailey saved her life."

Beau looked at Aaron and sat up straighter in his chair. Vampires didn't kill other vampires. It was a written law.

"It was justified. My house, my rules. Not to mention I carry a great deal of weight with the Vampire Council. And don't worry, Beau. You haven't done anything to warrant me killing you. Yet."

Beau was suddenly uncomfortable. He looked at the door and wondered what sort of excuses he could make to go back to Kyle's house. He wanted to be away before he did something stupid and this man had to remove his head.

Then he felt her, Megan, and his entire body tensed. She was upset, angry really, and he reached out to her only to find the connection blocked and then nothing. Beau swore ripely then flushed. He'd forgotten about the kids. "I'm sorry. I don't...I don't have a lot of occasion to hang out around kids and ladies. I just...she is...damn it all to hell and back." He stood up and began pacing. "She is gone again. How do I protect her when she...damn it." It was several seconds before Beau realized that the children and Sarah had left the room. He looked at the master and wondered what he would do with him.

"Sit down, Beau. Your mate, I presume? She is somewhat of a stubborn woman, isn't she? I have found myself wanting to strangle her myself."

Beau growled low in his throat. No man, especially not another vampire, touched anyone's mate. And Beau was just discovering how much he disliked having a mate. Especially one that didn't listen to him.

"Have a seat, Beau. We need to discuss your mate. I don't think she is all that happy about being a vampire and I believe that she is much more than she seems. What do you know about her?"

Beau nearly answered "nothing" when Aaron's cell phone rang. He pulled it out of his pocket and with an "I have to take this," he answered.

What did he know about Megan? Nothing was an understatement. She was beautiful, long dark hair, dark eyes that sparkled when she was aroused or pissed. He realized that she had been a great deal of both around him and he shifted in his seat. Megan was tall, though not overly so. A body that he would gladly worship, and do so hourly. A taste of her was as sweet as honey and as spicy as hot peppers. He wanted to bury himself in her and stay there. Beau looked over at Aaron and knew that he wouldn't be sharing any of that with the man. He scowled at the floor. Damn it, where was she?

"That was Thomas Reilly, my good friend and a damn fine doctor," Aaron started. "It seems your mate is employed at the clinic in the Merchant District with him and has been for several months. He informed me that she is a physician of good standing and that he has hired her on as the new doctor to work with him."

Chapter 10

The human was dead. Not that Samuel Rome cared, but he was still angry and needed more of an outlet for it. He strode over to the other man cowering in the corner and yanked him up by his hair. His neck snapped before Samuel could deliver the first blow. Tossing him across the room, he roared with frustration.

"She cannot thrall me any longer." Men scrambled to get out of his way as he made his way up from his sublevel. "I want her found, do you hear me? Found or I swear I will kill every one of you."

Samuel entered his office and threw himself in his chair. Three women immediately came in and draped themselves all over him. He was just in the kind of mood to kill them all, but held off. It was hard enough to get women to come to him easily, killing three or four because he was pissed would make it impossible. He stroked the hair of the woman closest to him.

"My lord, I have news."

He glared at Simon and, with only a raised brow, the houseman broke out in a profuse sweat. "It had better be good, Simon, or else it will not go well for you. Either make sure that it is or remove yourself from my sight."

Simon backed up a step then seemed to gather strength to take two forward. "The young miss, I believe I have information on her whereabouts. She is staying in the Master MacManus home."

Samuel bent his neck and the resounding pop made the girl on the floor next to him jump. Simon nearly bolted. Samuel might have thought it was funny if he wasn't so pissed. "I know that, you moron. What I don't know, and what I have asked you to find out, is why she is at his house, along with her name. When I sent that idiot Alfred to find her for me he was...never mind. Do you have an address for this MacManus person?"

Simon's head was bobbing now as he reached into a folder and brought out sheets of paper. He started to hand them to Samuel then stopped and began reading them to him. "She is reputed to be there with a male vampire. The male isn't known to the circles around the area, so I have surmised that he is either new to the area or a newly turned. Since the man MacManus is the master, I am assuming that he is newly turned. I have yet to learn his name or that of the young miss."

Her name had eluded him from the beginning, Samuel thought. Her beauty, however, he knew. When he'd seen her in the hospital one night while acquiring blood for his stash he'd seen her talking to Alfred. They had seemed friendly and Samuel had turned Alfred in the hopes he'd bring the girl to him. But that hadn't worked out either. Alfred had taken her, turned her, and then the idiot had met the sun.

With as much calm as he could manage, which wasn't a great deal, Samuel turned to the man before him, enunciating each word. "I want her name."

Simon turned and ran from the room. He would get it now or Samuel would happily kill him. It had been two years. Nothing, surely not something as simple as a name, could take two years to find.

Samuel cupped the woman's head that sat on the floor and brought her to his lap. Opening his robe, he pressed her mouth to his erection. When she whimpered he jerked her head up and glared down at her. "Take me or die. I want you to make me come down your throat. If you don't then I will find someone

74

who will and they'll do it over your dead body. Do I make myself clear?"

Nodding, she wrapped her hand around his cock. When her mouth slid over him he pulled one of the other women up and had her stand close enough that he could suckle her breasts and finger fuck her. He was not gentle with either woman.

Samuel wasn't a big man. His cock, even when fully erect, was barely five inches long and very thin, but that wasn't the point. The point was that he was mean, cruel really, and the women flocked to him for protection. He alone could keep them from certain death once they were brought to his house. If he didn't like someone or didn't think someone would be worth something to him, he would feed that person to his friends, quite literally.

Once he was finished, less time than he thought but forever to the women, they were sent from the room and he was left alone. He walked to the curtained wall and moved the panel hidden there out of his way. He descended the stairs until he was in the lowest part of the house. He walked over to the…the thing strapped there and shook him awake.

Snarling, it raised his head and looked directly at Samuel. His creation, he thought. *Mine and mine alone.* Smiling at it he pulled out the shirt he had found on Alfred.

"You must find her. I want her here and I want her unharmed. If you do this well, my son, I will reward you greatly."

Snarling again, the beast, for there was no other word for it, nodded once. Samuel walked to the far wall and stepped behind the enclosure and when the door was shut he opened the chain lock around the creature's throat.

It sprang at the enclosure, fangs long and sharp, his eyes red as blood. Samuel didn't flinch, he didn't so as much as move. If he was honest with himself, and he seldom was, he'd admit he was terrified of the beast. When the side door to this part of the house opened soundlessly the creature looked out into the field then back at Samuel. With a final snarl it leapt out the door and into the darkness. Samuel didn't move until he was sure the door was completely back into place. Then, with an unsteady breath, he walked back up the stairs and to his chamber. The sun would be up soon.

~~~

Megan finished her shift feeling lighter than she had in the last almost two years. She was exhausted and sore, her body felt battered and beaten, but she had worked as a doctor, a real doctor.

Thomas had given her a few small patients at first, a broken arm then a head wound. Then when he seemed satisfied that she wasn't a hack he left her alone to go about his business. In all honesty she was terrified at first and the more she did, the more she worked, the easier it became.

He had even given her an office of sorts. It had a hidey hole under the desk he'd told her, and there were some books, reference books on a small shelf along one of the walls. It had a computer on a tiny table and a plastic chair. There was also a toy-sized refrigerator and a microwave. The fridge had several bags of blood in it and she was happy to realize that she wouldn't have to take from someone here to keep up with the stress of working all night. She was nearly to the cave when she realized that after this she would be able to afford to get her car back.

The sun was just cresting when she saw Beau at the mouth of her cave and he didn't look any happier to see her than she was him.

"You left me. And you've blocked me all night. You aren't supposed to do that with a mate. How would I find you if something happened?"

She moved past him and into the cave without answering. Megan was not going to let him spoil her great mood. She knew he would follow her and she wasn't surprised to find him right behind her when she got in out of the light. It wasn't bright yet, but she could still feel it pull on her. "I'm tired and I need to die. Can't you just leave me alone? I was doing just fine before—

what the hell are you doing? Put me down." He had picked her up and thrown her over his shoulder. Before she could do anything more than yell at him they were in that bedroom again.

"First of all, you don't die when you sleep. It's a regenerative sleep that all vampires go into at some part of the day, usually the highest point of the sun. Secondly, you will stay here with me during that time. You are my mate and, as much as it pisses you off, you need me as much as I need you."

Megan started toward the door only to be picked up again and, this time, tossed on the bed. Before she could scramble off he was on top of her. His body felt really good there, but death, or this regenerative sleep he called it, was pulling her down.

"I can't fight you—"

"Good," Beau said with a slight chuckle. "That'll be a nice change. Now maybe I can get some rest. You've been blocking me. Why?"

She couldn't answer. Her body was slowly shutting down. Her eyes were heavy and her arms were leaden. Megan felt him move her, adjust her on the bed, but she couldn't make her body care enough to fight him. The last thing she remembered was him kissing her forehead.

Chapter 11

Mel was in the kitchen when Sara arrived. Duncan and Penny, the cook, were cooing over the new baby. Mel looked radiant.

Mel was the Queen of Magick. She was also Sara's cousin. The two women had been friends for years and though Mel lived in the Kingdom of Molavonta in another realm they got together as much as possible. More so since the new baby had arrived.

"My turn." Sara reached into the small crib and pulled the little boy into her arms. "Oh my, you're getting so big, aren't you, little guy?"

"He nurses like it's his life's work. And poops. Why didn't you tell me they only eat, sleep, and poop?" Sara looked at Mel and smiled. She didn't look the least bit upset by the duo of babyhood.

"Eventually they will add to their repertoire, but for now he's building you up to bigger and better things he can do." Sara looked down at the infant in her arms.

Years ago Mel had been pregnant. Her then mate, Sherman, had lured her into the sublevels of the castle. He set off an explosion that rocked the castle and caused the death of several men and women who were there to guard the queen. He also caused the loss of their child. It took a number of years for Mel to finally begin to live again and a few more before she met her true mate. Shamus was a true king to Mel's queen. And this baby was a result of that union.

Shamus James Phillip Xavier Keeper—though the keeper part was just used when humans were around. It was an inside joke between the women. Little Shamus was four months old and already showing signs of being very talented and extremely well behaved. Sara loved him to distraction. She looked up at Mel to tell her so and stopped. Something was wrong. "Mel?"

At a quick shake of her head Mel stood and took the baby from Sara. When he was in his crib a guard appeared and stood next to him. Mel didn't say a word to the man, but did look out the window and then came back to the table.

"We have to talk. Is Aaron up still?" They moved to the staircase as Mel spoke.

"Yes, he's in his...you're scaring me. What is it? What's happened? Shamus is all right, isn't he? Oh please, Mel, tell me."

They had stopped on the stairs just as Aaron came out of his study. He had felt her fear, Sara knew. As a bonded and mated couple he would feel everything she did. She looked up at him and he held out his hand to her. She went up the remaining steps to take it. The need to be held by him washed over her.

"Let's go inside there and close the door." Once they were in the office Mel continued. "Early this morning something was released in the human realm. I'm not sure where it came from precisely. By the time I felt it the thing was on the move. All I know is that its one focus is to come here."

Aaron pulled Sara onto his lap and she snuggled deep into his chest. The man could hold her like this and suddenly everything was all right. But now she could feel his fear as well.

"Do we know what, or should I ask who, it's coming for?" Sara looked at her mate and wondered what he knew. "And can it be killed?"

"I...I don't know the answer to the first question. I think it's a 'who,' female, but I can't be sure who yet. As for killing it? I'm not sure about that either. I can. But here, in this realm, it's hard to say what damage will be done or who it will harm on its way here. I was hoping…I would like to see the 'where' and the 'who' of it first."

"You want to see who sent it or who it's after? I can see the first part, but the second, aren't you just asking someone to be put in its path? Wouldn't it be easier to kill this thing, whatever it is, and then try to find out who sent it?" Sara shivered. This thing was coming to her home.

"Oh I know who sent it. Samuel Rome, a master vampire from somewhere out west. He helped create the thing centuries ago. I was told he had destroyed it, but obviously not." Mel got up to pace. "It was once human, a man of great strength and power. But the power corrupted him, destroyed his mind and his will to be anything but evil and a killing machine. Samuel took the man and made him into this…this thing. From my sources I've just learned that he kept it locked in the belly of the earth, hidden away until now."

Sara could see the hurt in Mel's face. "You knew the man before, didn't you? The man who had the power, you knew him."

Mel sat down on the sofa and looked at Sara, tears in her eyes. "Yes. He was a good friend long ago. Michael, his name is…was Michael. We grew up together. His power even as a child was amazing. He wasn't a true immortal, but he had found ways…magical ways, to keep himself young. Michael was the first boy I kissed, the first one who held my hand. He was my friend."

Sara went to her cousin and pulled her into her arms. Mel was hurting and probably felt a little responsible for what was going on. Sara looked over at Aaron who smiled softly at her.

"The person he is after is Megan, correct? And this master, it's more than likely the one I met the other night, the one I felt in my realm?" Mel nodded to both Aaron's questions. "I thank you for his name, by the way. Now we have to figure out why her, why Megan? He wanted the girl, said that she killed his child. He had to have known that she didn't kill her maker, a vampire can't. So why now, why her, and most importantly, what can she have that he wants badly enough to piss off the Queen of Magick?"

~~~

Beau woke first. Megan was still lying in the same position he'd put her in early this morning. She was beautiful awake, but more so in slumber. He moved the small strand of hair from her soft cheek.

Her face was so smooth that Beau found himself touching her again and again. The small slope of her nose fascinated him with its sprinkle of freckles and the small bump in the middle. There was a small scar on her lip, so tiny that he wouldn't have noticed it unless he was this close to her. He wondered where it had happened and then made a mental note to ask her sometime. Her full lips begged to be sampled. Running his thumb over them he found himself leaning down to taste them when he caught himself. He wanted to explore her first and kissing her would more than likely wake her. Grinning he continued something he knew that, once she was awake, he wouldn't be able to enjoy.

Beau knew that her eyes were soft; the color was so pale they made him want to beg her to open them for him. He wanted to see them again full of passion. The most he'd been able to view them was in anger and she did that very well. Looking down at her body he marveled at her size. When she was next to him, standing or lying down as she was now, she was so small, tall but tiny in frame. Her breasts he knew, were small but full and her nipples a dusty rose color that made him want to strip her down to see them again. He shifted closer and decided that he had waited long enough to taste her.

Beau gently touched his mouth to hers. Then he moved down along her jaw as he opened the first button down the front of her shirt. Kissing the exposed area as he opened more buttons he heard her soft moan and was encouraged enough to slide his hand down along the front of her jeans.

Her legs opened for him and he cupped her femininity. Another moan and he covered her breast with his mouth, soaking her shirt. Need coiled in his belly hard.

Opening her shirt all the way he took her bare nipple in his mouth and suckled the tip, worrying it while he rolled the other in his fingers. She moved closer to him and arched her back toward his mouth. Beau rolled over her and settled between her legs. Looking up at her face her eyes were wide open and dark with need.

"Please. I…don't stop. You make me feel…you make me feel." Her voice was soft, but husky and warm.

Sitting up on his knees, still between her legs, Beau pulled his shirt over his head and dropped it on the floor beside the bed. He reached down, unsnapped her pants, and lowered the zipper.

"I should make you pay for blocking me, but I can't. I need you too badly. Lift your bottom." When she did he pulled her pants and panties down her legs and moved to take them off completely. "You are beautiful, *mon amie*."

"I don't know what you mean by blocking you. You seem to be touching me. I don't understand. Oh yes, again."

He slid his finger inside of her and found she was wet and hot. He wanted to taste her more this time, run his tongue deep inside of her. Moving back on the bed he pressed his finger into her again until she was rising up off the bed with her feet planted on the mattress.

Leaning down, Beau buried his nose into the curve of her thigh. She smelled delicious. He wanted to bite her there, take her blood while she came, but he needed to taste her cream now, feel her come in his mouth.

Sliding in and out of her Beau suckled her clit into his mouth and groaned with her taste. Her essence was what he craved; the taste of her was more than he could have hoped for.

Moving his finger, he slid his tongue deep inside of her, fucking her with it like he would soon be doing with his cock. When her fingers wound in his hair he felt her press him closer to her. Sliding his hands under her he tilted her up so that he could take more of her into him and touch a part of her he wanted to be inside of almost as much as her pussy.

Her ass was tight; the puckered place was so tight he knew that she had never had a man there before. He was happy to be the first and the last. Pressing his thumb hard against it Beau was rewarded with a gush of hot cream for his effort. Megan moaned and tightened her thighs against his head. He wanted her to come, come hard and now. He tried reaching out to her on their mental pathway and found it blocked again. Lifting his head he looked up at her. "Come, *bébé*, come now."

Her scream of release was loud. He could feel her body tighten and then shatter as he took her again and again with his mouth. Sliding a finger into her ass and one into her pussy she came again. Beau could barely keep up with the copious amount of juices that poured from her body. When she was coming down again, her body jerking, he moved up her body and slid into her.

Beau knew he wouldn't last. He wanted to mark her again, taste her as he had before. When she slid her tongue along his pounding pulse at his throat he nearly came just from that. He wanted her throat, wanted to feel her hot blood pour down the back of his throat. Tilting her head, he was surprised by the bite of her fangs as they sank into him. His cock exploded inside of her; his climax roared out of him and deep into her. Lifting her wrist to his mouth, Beau bit, lust making him not careful with what he was doing. His bite was hard and he felt the vein rupture and blood spurt in him mouth. Clamping his mouth over the fresh wound, Beau drank greedily and long. He came again, pouring all of him into her body. He dropped his considerable weight onto her and then, with the last of his strength, he rolled to his side, taking her with him.

Neither of them slept this time. He lay there thinking of her ability to block him and held her to him. He knew she wasn't asleep. He could feel her fingers playing with the hair on his chest. He captured her hand when she made her way down his body toward his cock.

"*Non*, love. I am exhausted and we need to talk. You need to explain to me why you have not told me about you being a doctor and why you continue to block me." He wanted her again and wondered if there would ever be a time when he didn't. She was more than he had bargained for, yet exactly what he wanted in a mate. Well, sexually, that is.

"You keep saying that, that I'm blocking you. I don't know what you mean. Blocking you from what?" Megan sat up and rested her chin on her hand, which was on his chest.

"Your mind. We should be able to talk, hear each other's thoughts through our connection, the blood bond. But you are keeping me out. Why is that when I could help you with your needs?"

She sat up and sat cross-legged next to him. He was disappointed when she pulled the sheet over her lap, but he couldn't complain when she left her breasts bare for him. He rolled to his side and didn't bother with his own nudity. He wanted her again and didn't care if she could see that.

"You mean some sort of telepathy? I don't know what…that Dingdong person, MacManus, he did it. That night he took my blood." Beau didn't like that Aaron had taken from her, but was cut off before he could reply. "He cut me with my own knife and then took this tiny little bit of my blood and put it on his tongue. That's how he talked to me, huh?"

Beau knew that she was very unaware of what she was, but it seemed no one had taught her even the basics of being a vampire. He had to think back on how Kyle had told him then realized that the two of them, Megan and himself, were both orphans of a sort.

"Open your mind. Concentrate on relaxing it and let me see if I can get in." Beau closed his eyes. He could feel the wall; it was tight and very hard. He suddenly knew that it wasn't her. She wasn't blocking him, but someone else was. He looked at her and frowned.

"What? What did you find?"

He was distracted by her breasts for a second and then when she smacked him, he couldn't think about anything but the small bounce they did when she moved. Leaning forward Beau took her nipple into his mouth and suckled. Her moan and her fingers wrapping in his hair had him moving up and then pressing her down into the mattress again. He wanted her again. Now that he was over her he wanted nothing more than to rock into her and come. The knock at the door made him snarl. Her giggle didn't help.

"Whoever is there is going to be a dead man if the house is not falling down around us. Speak," he bellowed as he dipped again at her breast.

"It's Aaron and while the house isn't falling yet, it may soon. Come upstairs, the both of you. We have things to discuss." With another growl Beau moved to the side of the bed and sat up.

"I think I hate the man." And when Megan stood up and moved toward her clothes Beau pulled her into his embrace, resting his head on her belly. "Yes, I could gladly kill the man for interrupting us."

Chapter 12

Beau and Megan came from the lower levels not long after Mac and Lizzy came into the kitchen. Aaron loved his children and was excited about the new baby coming into the house. He reached over and laid his hand over the mound that was Sara's belly. The child within kicked against his hand.

As soon as Megan came through the door Mac turned to look at her. Aaron didn't say anything as his son got up and touched his hand to her chest. Aaron got up quickly when Beau made to shove his son away.

"Wait. He sees something we can't," Aaron whispered urgently. "Let him touch her, he won't hurt her." Aaron pulled the large vampire back and held him while still watching his son. "Mac is very good at his power. And he knows the rules of mates. He wouldn't do this if he didn't need to."

Aaron could feel the fury in Beau. It was strong and hot. Aaron had to commend the man, he didn't try to break free of Aaron, but let him hold him back.

"She is protected by someone. Someone…her maker. He protects her even in his death." Mac laid his hands on her head. "He blocks you from the one who would kill you. A creature he has…it took his life. This creature took your maker's life."

"Mac, who is the creature? Can you see him? What is he?" Mel shimmered into the room and spoke softly to Mac.

"He was once a great man. He didn't want to kill your maker, your friend." Mac looked at Megan as he answered Mel. "The creature told…Alfred that he didn't want to hurt you, that you were special and that Alfred would need to keep you safe. He told Alfred how to protect you even from himself."

Megan looked over at Beau. Terror was evident in her eyes and the set of her mouth. But she didn't move, she didn't brush Mac away as he studied her more.

"Can you tell me where the creature has been? Did he tell Alfred how to…how to kill him?" Megan asked as she put her hands over Mac's.

"Yes." Mac grinned. "He said the power is within you to set him free."

The adults adjourned to the living room after Mac and Lizzy were sent to bed. Aaron looked at Megan who seemed to still be in shock. Aaron couldn't blame her. He was sort of worried himself.

"This creature, I think…he's been in my head. I heard him, I guess you could say, the night that I met you." Megan pointed her finger at him. "I thought it was you, Aaron, and that you were going to hurt me or something."

Aaron moved to the fireplace and stood in front of it. "No. After I spoke with you I only kept tabs on you. That's how I knew that the man was in my realm. I wouldn't have bothered with him had I not felt your anger."

"Yeah, thanks for that. I still don't know why you butted in. I had it under control." Megan shifted on the couch when he came and sat down with her.

"You were asking him to kill you. I doubt that Beau would have been very pleased with me had I let that happen. Besides, I doubt he would have killed you right then. He wants you for something more. What, I don't know, but I don't think your life with him would have been all that easy."

Megan stood up and began pacing the room. Beau watched her with a hunger that Aaron could understand. He looked at his own mate and knew she could see it as well.

"That kid, Mac, he said that the power is within me to set him free. I don't know what he meant. Set who free? Was he talking about Alfred or this creature thing?"

Mel cleared her throat. "I would think them both. Michael is the creature's name. He was a good man, and somewhere deep within the creature he still lives. At one time he was a doctor; a healer I guess would be a better term. Sara said that you are a doctor as well. It could be that he knew that from Alfred when he killed him."

Megan didn't look convinced. Aaron decided that now would be a good time to tell her what she was, to give her a bit of a lesson in what she could do. He picked up the knife he had laid on the end table earlier and handed it to Mel. He knew it was the coward's way to do it, but he didn't want Beau to hurt him.

Mel took one look at the knife and then smiled. The knife was sailing across the room in a heartbeat. Beau was up and in front of Megan, but she shoved him behind her, caught it, and held it up as a weapon. No one moved for several seconds. Then Megan exploded.

"What the fuck! Are you nuts? You threw a knife at an unarmed woman?" They all looked at Beau who was standing behind Megan and breathing hard. "Are you growling? Oh grow up, I had it under control."

"A man protects what is his. You will obey me when I push you behind me and not try to protect me." His voice was calm, even low, but no one doubted the anger in it.

"I'm not yours. And the next time you say that I may have to hurt you. Go sit down, you overgrown ox." When Beau stood there without moving Megan walked away. "This was a test, I'm guessing. You know, I don't do well without cliff notes. The next time you throw a knife at me,"—the blade went through the air and landed a mere inch from Mel's hand resting on the arm of the couch—"you should make sure that I'm not as good with it as you are."

Aaron burst out laughing. He couldn't help it. It was the last thing he expected and the most perfect. She wasn't near as helpless or as defenseless as he had thought. He got up, pulled the knife from the wood, and handed it back to Megan. "You owe me for that. That was an expensive antique. But I'm glad to see you can use it. Here." Aaron handed her the knife, handle first. "Keep this. You may need it. It's silver."

Megan nodded and started pacing again. "I don't know why I'm so special. There are hundreds of doctors at the hospital. Why does he want me? I hadn't even gotten my results back when Alfred killed me so it couldn't be because I was a doctor yet."

"It could be because you are wolf, or at least part one. Somewhere in your lineage there was a were. And you being a vampire too could be what makes your blood stronger." Mel moved as she spoke. "You also smell like Michael. I'm not sure how, but I'll figure that out too."

It wasn't until Shamus shimmered in the room that Aaron understood. The baby. He was still nursing and probably wanted his mother. Mel moved to the big chair and turned her back to the room. Aaron looked over at Sara and smiled. He loved it when Sara nursed. His cock leapt at the thought of her swollen breasts then he realized he had missed a part of the conversation daydreaming.

"A wolf? I don't think so. My parents are as normal as they come. They would be...my parents would be really pissed if they heard you say that. Besides, I think I would have noticed them eating the gardener and howling at the moon."

Aaron was surprised at that. Her parents were still living. He had forgotten just how young a vampire she was. He wondered if that was a part of the reason this person, Rome, wanted her as well. He looked at Beau again. "You need to take her under your wing, so to speak. I'm assuming you've never shifted."

Megan looked at Aaron with a look of complete horror on her face. "You really do become a bat? Shit!"

"No, not unless I want to, that is. And I don't wear a cape either. Don't be obtuse," Aaron snapped. "You can shift into something, maybe several things for all we know. How did you survive all this time without some knowledge of what you can do?"

"I wasn't," Megan said softly. "Trying to survive, that is. I never wanted to be this monster, but I wasn't brave enough to end my life either. The first time the sun touched me was…I had to run and hide until I could heal. Do you have any idea what it's like to have your…I guess you do. But I didn't ask for this and I certainly don't want it."

"Megan, love, if you die so do I. You and I are a pair now, mated and bonded as a vampire couple." Beau started to reach for her, but she backed away. "Neither of us can feed from anyone else unless it's our maker. And that too is not an option for us. We are both orphans."

"No. No, I didn't bond with you. We only had…we only had sex. What are you talking about?"

Aaron was at once angry at Beau. He'd taken her and bonded with her without her consent. He started to rise, but Sara stopped him with a whisper through his mind.

"Had he not then she would surely be dead and we both know it. He may have broken the rules governing our kind, but she had made no bones about wishing her own death. Let them be, love."

"We have fed from each other during intercourse. To become a pair, we needed to have a climax together and exchange blood. It was easier with you than I would guess a human to vampire mating would be because you are already vampire." Beau let her go as he spoke again.

Megan looked terrified. Aaron watched her and wasn't surprised when she ran from the room, Beau fast on her heels. Aaron would have gone after them both, but Sara stopped him.

"She won't listen to you, love. She's more than likely not going to listen to Beau either. Let them go. They'll work it out."

"Or what? Kill each other? I think it's a good thing she can't hurt her mate. I think Beau is in for a long haul."

~~~

Michael watched the house. He knew that the female was in there. Her scent called to him. He moved closer, but not too close to the hum of electricity in the fence between him and her.

Michael paced in front of the gate, back and forth for several minutes. He was losing control of the beast that he'd become. If he was smart he'd go back to the house and he'd kill the man who dared to think he owned him, Samuel Rome, and then himself. Once he had a little more control over himself Michael went to the forest just behind the mansion.

He was a monster, nothing like the one that Megan thought she was, but real, horribly real. He'd been a man once, he thought, a good man, a man who could have been great. But he'd gotten greedy. He'd gotten a taste of what he'd made and let it go to his head. Michael knew what the consequences were to his experiment. But he thought he was beyond that, beyond the simple creatures that had turned vicious once the drugs had taken hold.

The formula was supposed to make it so that he could live forever. He had been an immortal, but he wanted more, needed more. He had played with the human body, cell research, blood typing and manipulations. Every test subject had been a failure until the end. Until the one man he'd tried it on. And Michael had thought he was ready to try it on himself.

It should have killed him. He wished every day that it had. He had created a new serum for immortality and had destroyed any chances of it working. He knew as soon as he was able he was going to destroy himself just as he'd done all his research.

Michael was slipping again. He could feel himself slipping away and the beast, the creature, taking him again. The transformation wasn't quick and it certainly wasn't without pain. As soon as he shifted Michael no longer existed.

Creature erupted from the human in a horrible shift of bones and muscle. He liked being in control and hated when the human fought him. Someday, and soon, he would be in control always. Someday very soon, the human would not be able to come out and play.

Creature moved along the fence and touched it with his claw. Sparks shot off the fence and had him jumping back in fear. He wished that Human would tell him things, let him know what he needed to do. But Human didn't like Creature; he only liked himself. Pissed off, Creature raked his claws along the tree and then moved to the road. His claws dug into the concrete, making a footprint that he hoped the human would see. Then she would know, she would know that it was useless to fight something so strong and come with him to the cage. He hoped that the blood man would let him play with her as he'd promised. He wanted to taste her blood as she died, drink from the puny human female that thought she could escape him.

Creature was starved. That was another thing that Human would do, starve him of meat. He loved meat. Creature would eat meat all the time if Human would just let him. Creature decided that he would have all the meat that he wanted when he was in control. All meat, all the time.

He knew that he couldn't get into the gate, it sparked too much for him, and that noise, the mean sound hurt his ears. He snarled at it again and left the area. He could smell her now, the female. He wanted to pull out the shirt again that the blood man had given him, but his claws were too long and the human stuff, the material, wasn't on him any longer.

Creature moved along the perimeter of the fence following the scent. It was faded and hard to follow, but creature knew he would find it again and he did. Over and over he found it to follow. He was inside of the cave before the sun rose and he could smell her now. It was strong and Creature liked it. He marked the area so that no others would come here, his scent strong to show her that he was strong. Burrowing deep in the earth Creature lay down to wait. She would return, and when she did Creature would have her.

Chapter 13

"Damn it, will you wait a second? You're going to get us both killed if you don't stop."

Megan turned to look at the man who she wished would just go away. "I didn't ask you to come with me. In fact, I would be just as happy if you would go the fuck away."

"I'm not leaving you. We need to talk about this. You need to know that—"

She turned on him and advanced quickly at him. "I need to know? What I need to know is why you did this to me. Why you think I should be thrilled that you turned me into your food tray. Where do you get off…oh, forget it."

She turned again to leave him when he grabbed her arm. When she spun around to face him she had her fist doubled up and caught him in the jaw. It hurt like hell, but she managed to make him let her go. It was short-lived, but she did feel a moment of triumph. But only a moment.

The second time he grabbed her he was prepared and she missed him by a good foot. She didn't know if she was happy she missed because her hand hurt, or pissed because she missed because now he had her again. When she ended up on his shoulder she couldn't see for several seconds until she tried to sit up using his back as leverage.

"Put me down, you moron. I can't see. If you don't put me down this—" His hand came down on her ass painfully. "You are so going to pay for that. When you put me down, I'm going to hurt you badly, buddy."

"Be still. I didn't hurt you, *mon amour*. I can smell your arousal even now. We will talk if I need to hold you here for the rest of the night." Megan watched as he started to walk. He would, too, she thought. He'd carry her all night.

"Now, what is this nonsense about you not enjoying the way we bonded? Was it not good for you? I can try again if you would like. It will be very little hardship on my part."

No doubt, she thought. "Put me down. You're making me sick to my stomach. And as much as I would relish puking down your back, you'd probably make me clean you up."

"You will behave?"

She nodded then realized he couldn't see her. "Yes. As long as you don't try to have sex with me again, I will. Otherwise, all bets are off." She slid down his body. Her breath caught when she was pressed against him. Her feet didn't quite touch the ground, but she could touch his feet. His mouth was very close, close enough that she could see the tips of his fangs as they touched his lower lip.

"You want me, do you not? Your scent is making my beast rise with need. Do you feel how badly I want you, *mon amour*?"

She could too. His cock was swollen and hard against her. Megan nodded as she watched his mouth lower to hers. He was going to kiss her and she knew that she was going to let him. The loud howl in the distance broke them apart and they had their backs to each other.

"You must ob...listen to me, please. We are out in the open and we could be harmed. I care not for myself, but I will not allow you to be where someone can take you from me."

"Because you can't live without me, right? You'd starve so having me living is all you can do?"

As soon as the words left her mouth, she knew they weren't true. He had done nothing to her that she didn't want as badly as he did. She felt him stiffen behind her and nearly turned to tell him she was sorry.

"No. You must stay there until we are certain the beast is gone. But know this, Megan Reed, I need you in my life for more than food. I have fallen in love with you and your stubborn ways and sarcastic words."

"Gee thanks. Be still my heart." His chuckle had her wanting to smack him, but the howling started again. Aaron appeared before her.

"Shit. Don't you knock or something? There's a beast out there and you're sneaking up on me."

"Oh," Aaron started, a bite to his tone. "Next time I feel your terror I will make sure I send you a telegram first. That way you'll know, as well as the monster in the forest will know, that I'm coming. Come on. Bradley said that it's in the caves just ahead."

Megan had the most irresistible urge to giggle. Dingdong was really pissed and she would probably piss him off more if she did. But she couldn't help it. He was a nasty bastard when he wanted to be. When he suddenly stopped she ran into his back.

"I can smell it now. Can either of you?"

Megan sniffed the air. She couldn't smell anything at first. Beau coming up behind her had her tense for a second until he began to show her what to do.

"You must find what you do not know. Find the things you are aware of, that smell like the things you have scented before, and take those away. Separate them from each other. Find the one that is different."

Megan started to separate the different odors like he had said. She took out the two men beside her. Then the scent of the night, first the forest's loam and the dried leaves. Next, the animals she knew, the wolves and the mice and other small animals. Soon she was left with a scent. It wasn't strong, but there. "It's them. The beast that howled tonight is there, and a man with him. The man, he is with him some, but not always." Megan sniffed again and then leaned down closer to the dirt. "But it isn't two men, I think. Something is...he has two separate smells because he has changed." Megan looked up at Aaron and at Beau. They both looked surprised if not a little impressed. She actually felt pretty good herself.

"That makes sense if you think about it. One man who can shift into two different beings. Isn't that how a shifter does it to hide his scent?" Megan looked at Aaron as he spoke, then at Beau. She knew he was hiding something from her.

"But you know that's not all, don't you? What aren't you telling me? Please, I have a right to know."

Beau nodded and turned to Aaron. "It's her. He smells like Megan when he's in human form."

~~~

Beau didn't like this. Not at all. After they'd gone back to the mansion they had sat for another few hours going over what they had discovered. Bradley had said that the creature had gone to the caves where his pack could smell both Megan and the beast. When they had entered the lair the beast was not there, but he had torn up her things.

Everything Megan had had been destroyed. Books and papers, even her clothes had not been spared. She had run to the back of the cave, pulled up a large stone, took out a smallish chest, and sat and wept over it until he had had to pick her up and bring her to the house. She hadn't said much since then. He was worried she might snap, more worried that she didn't fight him back when he'd deliberately picked a fight with her four times now.

Aaron and Sara had told him she would be fine, that she was strong of mind and she needed to deal with this in her own way. Sara told him that he couldn't help her with this sort of grief, but everything within him wanted to try. When Megan finally stood up and handed him the book he reached for her hand and held it.

"My parents...my mom and dad, they have to know what's going on. I have to tell them what I am and ask them what they know."

Her voice broke his heart. She sounded so defeated and hurt. He looked down at the book again then back up at her. He flipped open the first page and was surprised to find a photo album.

There were pictures, hundreds of them. An older couple standing alone and several of them with a child. Beau saw that the child, a little girl, looked like Megan. Lifting it to the light better he realized it was her. His Megan was a chubby little thing. When Megan put her finger on the page and he looked at what she was pointing at he knew they were her parents.

"I never looked like them. Never, even as a child. And they were so much…" Her voice caught. "They were so much older than the other parents when they had meetings. I'd never been in trouble, but they would come to the open houses and the parent meetings."

"I don't understand. You were just a little fat baby, nothing more. Tell me what you're trying to say, love."

"I asked them once why there was only me. Momma told me it was because they had been blessed with me. She didn't say that she couldn't have any more children, but that she and Daddy had been blessed."

Aaron cleared his throat. "You think you were adopted by them." He didn't say it as a question, but as a statement of fact.

"No. I think I was placed with them. There was no record of my birth. When I started school the teacher kept asking them for it. Every day for two weeks I'd bring home a note. Then late one night I heard my momma crying on the phone. The next day, Mrs. Mann was gone and someone else was in her place."

"Why would you think you were placed with them because a teacher disappeared? That doesn't make any sense."

Megan took the book from him, flipped through pages, and then handed it back to him. "That's my uncle. I'd never met him before that day. Look at him, Beau. Really look at him."

Beau put the book under the light again to get a better view. He had excellent eyesight, but wanted to please her by making sure he didn't miss any details. He was about to hand it back to her when he saw it. A wolf just behind them in the shadows not a foot from her and her uncle. Beau looked up at Megan.

"The wolf was there off and on all day. She would disappear if my parents came out and return when they would wander off. My momma said that it was a dog. That she had taken the picture and she knew it was a dog."

"Couldn't it have been? I mean, it's not a great picture, but it could be, I suppose."

Megan was already shaking her head at him. "She didn't take the photo. I told you the wolf would disappear when they came around. The picture was taken by another wolf, one that shifted into a man to take the picture for me. He said his name was Michael."

Chapter 14

Megan didn't wait for the sun to set before she ran upstairs. She wanted to talk to Sara before everyone else was up. The shades that drew tight over the windows were still down in the house when Megan walked into the large room they had called the half room. Sara and the children were sitting on the couch watching the television.

"Megan. I didn't expect to see you for another hour. If you want to talk to Aaron, he's—"

"No, you. I need to talk to you. It's about this bond thing. Is there a way to break it?" Megan had given it a great deal of thought. She was in danger if the attacks were any indication and the sooner she broke it off with Beau, the sooner he could get on with his life. He enjoyed begin a vampire, she didn't. This was the best possible way. She and Sara entered the large study and when she shut the door Sara sat as she asked Megan why.

"Why would you want to? I mean you seem happy with Beau. I know that the two of you have bonded. Is it the half-breed thing? If it is then we—"

"No. No, that's not it. He..." Megan began to pace again. "He seems like an okay guy. I mean, he's a bit stiff about stuff, but nothing I can't get around. It's that I don't want to be here. No, that didn't come out right. I don't want to be a vampire. I want to be...well, dead." Megan knew that she shocked the woman, but her stand on honesty had always been "go with it." If someone didn't want to know the answer, then that person should think before he or she asked the question.

"I see. No, actually, I don't see. Why not? And I don't mean Beau, though I think he'd be pissed for a lot of reasons about this conversation. But why don't you want to be a vampire?"

Megan was afraid she'd want answers. Megan had some, but she was sure that they weren't the ones that would get her what she wanted. If she was honest with herself she wasn't all that sure what she did want. "That man, or beast, or whatever, do you think he's going to stop until he gets whatever it is he's after? And what do you think he's going to do with me once he gets me? Because I have to tell you, Mrs. Mac, I don't think he's going to be inviting me over for a nice cup of tea, do you?"

Sara snorted and that made Megan laugh. "No. But do you think that Beau is simply going to let you walk out of his life? I doubt it. Are you, Beau?"

Megan turned to the door. She never heard it open and was sure that was the point. Beau looked pissed, more than pissed actually. He looked like he wanted to strangle her. Megan backed up several steps when he came toward her.

"Running from me now is not an option, Megan. I'm not happy with you at the moment and it will go so much better for you if I do not have to chase you as well."

She didn't stop; she wasn't stupid. "What are you going to do to me? I only had your—" She hit the wall behind her. "Beau, you have to know that you could be hurt if I don't do—"

"Quiet, woman. Sara? I was wondering if you would please tell the master that I will be detained? That I have some...disciplining to do."

Megan looked at Sara who stood up. "She doesn't have to leave. This is her office, you know, and her house. Yeah, it's her house and you shouldn't make a woman leave a place that technically belongs to her. Isn't that right, Mrs. Mac?"

Sara smiled. Megan didn't like that smile and was reasonably sure that she wasn't going to like what she said and, even worse, what Beau had planned for her.

"I don't mind. I think my work here is done anyway. See you downstairs later, Beau. Megan, this is for the best." And with that, she was out the door.

Megan looked up at Beau when she heard the lock click into place. The best for who, she wondered?

Beau pulled her toward him then sat on the couch. When she started to sit next to him he pulled her across his lap with her ass in the air. He was so not going to spank her.

"You lay one hand on my ass and I will hurt you, you overgrown ass." His hand hit her ass seconds after she finished her threat. "Damn it, that fucking hurt. Let me up." His hand smacked her again.

Struggling only made it worse, she realized, and tried to lay still. That was when she noticed his erection. It was hard against her belly and it was all she could do not to shift over him. She was pissed, damn it, and wasn't going to be turned on by this act of meanness.

"You drive me insane, Megan. You will not"—his hand came down again—"go behind"—then again—"my back again." Another blow, not just to her ass, but to her pride.

"Let me up." Megan was fighting tears and she would not let him see that he'd hurt her. He didn't move his hand from her after the last blow and she started to struggle. He held her still with a hand to her thigh and her lower back.

"Shhhh. Let me sit here for a moment, *mon amour*."

His hand started to caress her, gentle now on her tender bottom. The pain was gone and in its place was…arousal. She started to struggle again when he slid his hand under the waistband of her pants.

"It is hot. And soft. Does it hurt?" She felt herself arch up into his hand as he slid his finger into the seam of her ass.

"Don't. I'm mad at you. You whipped me." His soft chuckle had her pissed all over again and she tried to get away.

When he pressed his finger deep into her rosebud she moaned. It was pain and pleasure both and, damn him, she wanted more.

"You say you are mad, but I can feel you are enjoying this." His finger moved in and out of her over and over again. "I will take you here. Soon, I think. I will fill you with my cock and make you scream with your release."

She wanted to tell him he was full of shit, that he'd never do those things he said, but they would both know it for what it was—a lie. When he moved her off his lap she whimpered a bit. But he soon had her lying over the arm of the couch, her ass in the air, and he was reaching around her waist and undoing her pants.

Panting hard, she couldn't even help him. Her body was on fire for his. When he had her pants down around her thighs she arched back against his mouth as he rained kisses over her tender cheeks. On all fours, she turned to look back at him over her shoulder. He was gorgeous, powerful, and hers. "Beau, please. I need you. Please?"

"I need you as well, my heart. And I will have you. First, I must taste you." Putting words to action she came immediately when his tongue entered her pussy.

Megan couldn't catch her breath. While her body was still tight with her climax Beau entered her ass again with his clever finger. His tongue danced inside of her and his fingers stretched her, widening her as he pressed another, then another into her. He was burning her up from the inside out. The pain of him inside her virginal hole soon gave way to incredible pleasure. Her climaxes, one on top of the other, ripped through her, over her, and into her. Megan was sure she would never survive this. With every move into her Megan arched back toward him. When he pulled away she cried out. Needing him more than she ever thought possible she turned to beg him to please not stop and caught him undressing.

He looked up at her when she moaned. His eyes had turned, as had hers; she could see him through a tint of red haze. His shirt was off, he had already pulled his pants open and his cock, still hidden from her, strained against the silk of his boxers.

Licking her suddenly dry lips Megan watched as he reached into his boxers and stroked himself. She wanted to watch him, see his cock, but knew that if she begged he wouldn't give her any more of himself until he was ready.

"I am hard for you. My cock aches to spread you wide and fill you." Megan watched him, her body canting to his strokes. "You are wet, dripping with need."

"Please, Beau. I want to come with you inside of me." She was going to come as soon as he touched her; she knew it was just a matter of when, not if.

He moved up behind her and spread her cheeks; his cock nudged at her entrance. Her pussy contracted at the contact. When his finger entered her again she nearly came up off the couch. His cock nudged her harder.

"Please," Megan begged, then he slammed into her hard and quick. "Oh God, yes."

He gripped her hip with his free hand and pulled her tight against him. Over and over he pounded in her, twice, three times she came, screaming out his name and cursing him too. When he leaned over her, both his arms trapped her between them and he pistoned deeper, harder, faster. Megan laid her head on the armrest and let him. The first spray of his cum brought her again. Then he jerked her up so that they were both on their knees. And still deep inside of her, he tilted her head and took her throat.

~~~

Beau wasn't sure he'd ever be able to move again. He had never been like this with another woman, needing to conquer, to take. He sealed the tiny prick marks at her neck and held her to him. Her body shook and tightened around him. He wasn't sure if it hurt or felt wonderful, but he couldn't pull away.

"Are you all right, *mon amour*? I didn't mean to…well, I did mean to hurt you, but only with pleasure."

She laughed and his heart sang. "Then you succeeded. I think you might have ruined me for anyone else."

Beau growled deep in his chest. "There will be no other, *cœur de la mine*. It will only be you and I for all of eternity. You cannot leave me. I will...I will meet the sun even if you manage to get our bond broken. You are my life and I cannot...no, I will not, live without you."

She leaned back against him and he held her to him. He could hold her this way for all their days together. When she sighed heavily Beau sat back on the couch and pulled her into his lap.

"He means to kill me, you know that, right? And if killing me isn't in his plan, he will have to before I submit to him. I won't go easily."

He had to laugh knowing full well that she wouldn't. She turned to look up at him. Her forehead was marred by her frown. He reached out and caressed it with his thumb. "Do not worry. I will not let anything happen to you. You and I, we will—"

A scream rent the air then a loud thud and shattering glass. Megan leapt up and yanked on her pants as Beau did the same. He was terrified that someone had broken into the house and when someone screamed again, this time female, Beau stopped then moved to the now open doorway.

They were both out the door as they still were pulling on clothes. The first thing Beau noticed was the broken rail that separated the long hallway upstairs from the open way of the entrance downstairs. Leaning over and looking down his heart stopped beating for several seconds. A child, Mac, lay there in a pool of blood.

Chapter 15

Aaron couldn't move. He simply shut down. He knew that someone was saying his name over and over, but he could not get his mind to work at what was being said. Then suddenly a stinging slap woke him. He glared at Megan.

"You had better—"

"Focus. I need you to get me a sheet and rip it into strips. Duncan, there is a medical bag in the bedroom where I was with Beau. I need it."

"I'll get it. I can move faster." Beau moved out of the room and Aaron still stood.

When she drew back her hand to hit him again Aaron caught it. "Once was quite enough. The sheets are on their way. I need to know…my son…is my son…"

"I will do everything I can. You have to listen to me. I'm going to…I have to move him off the glass, but I don't know anything about his kind. Will he bleed to death if I can't get the bleeding to stop?"

Sara whimpered again and Aaron saw that Mel had shimmered into the room and took her away. Aaron was torn between wanting to go with her and staying with Megan. But she was right, he needed to help her.

"He'll bleed to death. He isn't at his majority yet, twenty-five. He isn't twenty-five yet. He has fourteen more years then he won't bleed out." Aaron was babbling, but he couldn't seem to help himself. He didn't want to look at Mac, but he turned when Megan turned toward him. Mac was…he knew his son was dead.

"Mr. Mac, you need to listen to me. I need you to focus or I don't know what to do. Mac is different than you. I mean other than the vampire thingy, he's different. What is he?"

"Necromancer. He talks to the dead and helps them. He's really quite good at it for someone so—I'm doing it again, I'm sorry." He needed to shut up. But talking seemed to make the terror less.

"No problem. Take his hand and hold him. I'm going to tourniquet his leg." Beau handed her a bag. "It looks like he's severed his artery. I need to stop the blood flow and then I'll work on the other things. All right?"

Was it? He didn't have a clue. He nodded because he wasn't sure what else to do. Taking his son's hand in his, Aaron felt the coldness of it and wanted to weep. When Megan told him to talk to his son, Aaron started telling him how terrified he was and stopped.

"No, tell him. He needs to know that you care, that you love him. I want you to lie here next to him and speak to him. Keep it up, he can hear you."

Aaron did as he was told. He lay in the blood because they hadn't moved him yet. And he talked. Aaron started out telling Mac about his birth. "You were so bruised. Your neck was black and blue, but still the most beautiful thing I'd ever seen. I'll be honest with you, son, I was terrified to hold you. Afraid I'd hurt you somehow. But your Aunt Pete just shoved you in my arms like I was supposed to know what to do. I suppose I did after a fashion." He could hear them talking. At some point, Thomas had come in. Aaron saw him and that he and Megan worked well together, but he didn't stop talking. "Then there was the time you had to be sent home from school. Fighting, they said. I knew you wouldn't do what they had said so I sat you down and asked you questions. Do you remember that? I got to the bottom of it, as you remember. You were protecting our Lizzy, you told me. That bully had tried to hurt your little sister and you weren't standing for it. I'd never been so proud of you before."

Aaron heard Megan shouting at someone, but he wasn't sure who. Aaron squeezed Mac's hand and thought about his first bike ride. "I didn't want you to learn how to ride it. But your mother insisted. She said that every young boy and girl needed to learn to ride a bike. I would never tell her this, but she was right. I think it was more that I myself didn't know how to ride and was afraid you'd ask me to go riding with you. You didn't, though. I wonder if you knew somehow."

"Mr. Mac. I'm going to move him now. We've stopped the bleeding in his leg. We need to take him to the clinic and operate there. The ambulance is here."

Aaron didn't let go of his son, but held him. "I can take him quicker. If you can meet me there, I can get him there quicker."

Megan nodded. "Thomas can go that way. I'll just ride with your wife in the—"

"No. No, you'll come with us. I need you there. You've seen him this far…Thomas, tell her. Tell her that she needs to be there."

"Mr. Mac, I can't do that thingy. I don't have a clue how to move like that. I can come—"

"I said no. Beau, take her, please. I need her there. You'll bring her with you, please?" Aaron wasn't used to begging anyone, but he knew that his son would live because of her. "Please, Megan, he's my little boy."

"All right. I'll come with Beau. You take him there and we'll be right behind you, I guess. You're doing fine, Mr. Mac. Just fine."

Aaron shimmered in the hospital seconds later. He didn't want to put Mac down, but the staff seemed to be ready for him and he had no choice. Mac was rushed away before he could tell him anything else. Aaron felt someone come up behind him and was startled to see Colin and his mate Shade.

"He fell. Mac is hurt and I…I…" Suddenly, he was engulfed in massive arms.

Colin hugged like he did everything, with all of him. Aaron didn't want to pull away. He hadn't realized how much he needed this until he had it. Tears welled in his eyes. Sara and Mel were there seconds later along with Beau and Duncan.

"I brought her. She's with Thomas. I went back for Duncan. He wanted to be here too," Beau said before Aaron could ask him.

"Yes, of course. Duncan is his honorary grandfather; of course he'd want to be here. We should sit. I'm going to go and check on him. I'll be—"

Another couple came into the room then another. Pete and Dominic and also Tristan and Bailey. Aaron was so overcome with emotion that he had to take several breaths before he trusted himself to speak. But Sara seemed to know and pulled him into her arms.

"You have no idea how much we needed you all here. We can't thank you enough for this. Mac would be so embarrassed by all this fuss."

Aaron saw Lizzy and went to her. Mac's twin would feel his pain more than any of them and his little girl seemed so small sitting there. Aaron pulled her in his lap and held her like he had when she was small.

"He's in good hands, love. Very good hands. Megan is a great doctor. I have heard so many good things about her and if Mac can make it, she'll help him."

~~~

Megan worked like she never had before. The lacerations in his thigh had cut through his vein and he had been losing blood quickly. She tried not to think of the vibrant little boy she knew and instead kept her focus on his wounds and saving him. Megan had ignored the man lying next to him at the house, but not the woman in the other room. Sara's cries had been driving her insane. It wasn't until Thomas put his hand on her shoulder that she calmed down.

"She's hurting as well. You can do this, Megan. Keep breathing and you will save him. I have no doubt and neither should you."

Now they were in the operating room. She had just closed up the wound on his leg and was stretching when Thomas winked at her over his mask. "Got a good set of hands on you, girl. I think I might keep you for myself. Where'd you learn to stitch like that?"

"I have no idea. I've never done more than sew up a couple of knife wounds before tonight. And set a few bones, but never anything on this scale." She was dizzy now and staggered to the wall.

"Forgot about that, you being a new vampire. You must feel the sun coming up. Let me get Beau for you. He'll see to your needs." Thomas stopped just outside the operating room. "You did a good job, Megan. Nobody else would have been able to save that kid but you. Once he gets a little blood in him, he'll be good as new."

She watched while they put wrappings around him and then wheeled Mac out. She must have fallen asleep because the next thing she knew Beau was picking her up in his arms.

"Hi. I'm really tired. Just put me in a dark room and I'll be fine." Megan couldn't hold her eyes open. "I think he'll be all right, don't you?"

Beau tightened his hold. "Yes. He'll be fine. Thomas said you did a good job, that you saved him."

"Thomas is over exaggerating. He was right there too." Megan closed her eyes again. "Beau, will you let me sleep with you tonight?"

"Yes, *mon amour*. Tonight and every night."

She heard him and wanted to comment, but it was too much. Weak and tired, she didn't fight it any longer. Sleep claimed her long before they were in his bed.

Chapter 16

Megan wasn't in the bed when he woke up. Beau was irritated to say the least and got up. He spotted the note as soon as he turned on the light.

"Beau,

Mr. Duncan took me back to the hospital. I needed to check on Mac. I hope I can be back before you get up, but if you're reading this, I wasn't able to be. Mr. Duncan lent me his cell phone. You can call me if you want to.

Megan"

If he wanted to? What he really wanted to do was cuddle next to her and make love to her, but he could almost understand that she would need to see her patient. He thought about what had happened yesterday and what Megan had done to save the master's child.

She had saved him, there was no doubt of that. But it was how she had done it that amazed him. She had leaped over the railing, landing like a cat, and was beside the child before Beau had been able to get there. He doubted that she was even aware of what she had done.

Beau made his way up the stairs without much hope of finding anyone at home, fully prepared to go to the hospital to be with her. He was surprised to find Mel and her mate Shamus there with little Lizzy.

"They're all at the hospital. I've come to be with Lizzy and to try to keep the home fries burning." Beau grinned at Mel.

"Its home fires burning, love, not fries," Shamus told her with an affectionate pat on the head. "Mac is doing well. Megan is with him, as are Aaron and Sara. Thomas cannot stop telling everyone how she saved Mac. Megan is hiding from him. He keeps dragging her around the place and showing her off as his find."

Beau didn't like that much, but didn't say anything. He sat in the chair next to Lizzy and winked at her. "How you holding up, kid? Your brother was pretty lucky."

She nodded. "He talked to me last night in his sleep. We can do that, talk to each other without being in the same room. Momma said it's because we're twins. She's probably right. Momma is always right."

Beau grinned at her. "I'm sure she tells you that a lot, hum?"

Lizzy grinned back at him. "Yeah, that's how I know it's true. Megan said that she didn't know how she saved Mac. She said she'd never done anything like that before."

Beau thought Lizzy might have misunderstood and let it go. Megan knew what she was doing; there was no doubt in his mind. She was just too skilled at it not to be. Beau was quite proud of his mate for what she had done.

He went to the hospital soon after Lizzy went up to her room to take a nap. She wanted to be able to be up when her parents got home.

There were a lot of people still hanging around the waiting room. He didn't see Megan or the MacManus', but when he asked a nurse she led him back to a room. He could hear voices before he opened the door.

"Don't be stupid, Megan. Of course we don't care. Call them. If they don't want to answer your questions I'll have Aaron go over and drain them for you." Beau could hear the humor in Sara's tone, but had no doubt that she would do it.

"No thanks. I think we'll try that one next, if they don't help me because I called. Okay?"

Beau walked in just as Megan was pacing the room. She was beautiful and Beau wanted her now. He walked over to her when she turned to look at him. "Hi, mon *amour*. You were not in bed when I woke. How is your little patient today?" Even though he had whispered he knew that both Sara and Aaron had heard him.

"Hi. Look, Mac is awake."

He had to work at it, but he managed to tear his eyes from Megan. She was all he wanted and more.

"Hello, Mr. Beau. Megan was just telling us about her parents. They aren't so nice people. I think you should go over and beat them up."

"Hum. Maybe you should get better so that you may join me. I could always use another man to help me with the infidels."

Sara groaned. "You should have heard his father. Beau, don't encourage him. I just...he's my little...I'll be back."

Sara sped out the door before Beau could say anything. He looked at Aaron then at Megan. They both looked sad.

"I'm sorry, master. I didn't mean to upset your mate. I was only kidding with the child. I thought to make him laugh."

Aaron stood and went to the door. "Don't worry about it, Beau. She's just still upset about the fall. And the baby is making her hormones all over the place. I'll be right back."

Megan sat in the chair next to the bed. She looked so good sitting there that Beau wanted to scoop her up and make use of the other bed. He realized she was speaking to Mac and decided to try and curb his hunger for her. He grinned when he thought about getting her home with him.

"I can handle my parents, but I thank you for offering. I'm going to call them soon. I have lots of questions for them."

Beau lifted Megan up and then sat her on his lap. Mac laughed. He knew the boy would be used to seeing couples touching and holding each other. Sara and Aaron were always touching each other. Megan, however, wasn't quite so receptive.

"Put me down, you idiot. What's the matter with you? Stop that." She smacked his hand when he started to rub her arms up and down. He wanted to pull her tighter against him to show her how much he wanted her, but knew the exact moment she figured it out. He shifted in the seat when she moved. His cock hurt it was so hard.

Beau wanted to grab her up and take her to the nearest dark private room, but he knew that she was exhausted. Her hunger beat at him as well. He was about to tell her...no, ask her to come with him when he felt it. Someone was in his mind uninvited.

With a quick look around the room he realized it was just the three of them; Mac, Megan, and him. He knew that anyone within the building could have been responsible, but somehow knew that it wasn't. Then he spoke to Beau, whispered through his mind.

"Do you love her?" Beau knew it was male. He wasn't sure how he knew, but he was positive of that. *"Do you love her, vampire? It's a simple question."*

"She's my mate. Who are you and what do you want?" Beau demanded of the voice.

"Yes. She is your mate, but you didn't answer the question." Before he could, the voice went on. *"She needs a mate. She was meant for greater things. But you...we'll get to that in a bit. You're a vampire. Not an old one, but strong."*

Beau shivered and smiled at Megan. He wasn't sure if she could hear the person or not and didn't want to alarm her.

"No, she's unaware. I have waited for a time when you and she were together when you weren't having monkey sex." Laughter rippled in Beau's mind. *"I love that description of sex. And so apt to what happens between two people who enjoy it."*

Embarrassment made him angry. *"What do you want? Who the fuck are you?"*

The male didn't answer right away. Beau wasn't sure, but he felt humor, not anger as he had expected in return for his outburst.

"The girl is my niece. I do not know her name and it is best that I do not. For now at least. Tonight I will visit you if the beast does not rise. You will not speak to him if he contacts you. It is best that you do not let him take the girl. He will without a doubt kill her." Beau felt him moving from his mind.

"Wait. The beast…you called him the beast. I need to know who he is and what he is to my mate." Beau had caught himself before saying her name. He knew how magic worked; a name meant everything.

Anger boiled through Beau, heating his body and mind in a haze of anger and a killing rage. Beau felt his own body react; his fangs dropped for battle and he pulled Megan tighter against him. The voice, when it spoke again, was harsh and hard, low and mean.

"I am Creature. Creature has great strength and great power. I am a great beast. Creature will destroy you, destroy man who dares take me over." Then in the voice soft from before, *"We are one, the Creature and I. Save her."*

Chapter 17

Megan felt there was something wrong with Beau, but she wasn't sure what. He'd been acting strangely since they'd left the hospital. She knew he was distracted; he'd been speaking to her in French for the better part of an hour. She thought she'd see if he was listening as well.

"So, I thought once we got back to your place, I'd jump your bones. Have my wicked way with you." He merely nodded and gave her a short grunt. "Then I thought I'd take your cock into my mouth. I've never enjoyed that before. But with you I might. Do you think you'd enjoy that, Beau?"

"Sure, *mon amour*. Anything you say."

He sounded like he was answering a small child, she thought. "You could come down my throat. I think that would be delicious. All that hot, spicy cum." Her fun was starting to backfire, she realized. What she was saying was starting to turn her on. "My own juices would be hot too, dripping down my thighs. My nipples are hard, my breasts are swollen. You could bite me there. Take your nourishment from my breast. Suckle me. I would ride your cock as you did it, hard and fast." She looked up when she realized that he was breathing hard.

"What are you saying, Megan? Do you really wish me to do those things to you? Take your blood that way?"

Megan wasn't sure at what point he'd tuned into her, but she had his full attention now. She was suddenly glad that

119

someone else was driving and that the limo provided them with privacy. Instead of answering, she moved across the seat and straddled his hips. With her legs on either side of his, she brushed her lips to his. Beau cupped her ass and brought her closer to him, to his heat.

His moan made her brave, made her bold. She canted her hips over his and ran her hands down his arms to his hands. She lifted them and put them behind his head. Megan was thrilled when he laced his fingers and relaxed more into the seat beneath her.

"You wish to take me, *mon amour*? I will be a willing subject for you. To a point. But our destination is nearly done and you have the look of a woman who would take her time with a man. Is that what you wish?"

"Yes. But I can't wait to taste you, Beau, to feed from you. May I? May I drink from you, please?"

He tilted his head, exposing his throat to her. His eyes, dark now with passion and his own hunger made her juices gush from her, the scent strong in the back of the car. Leaning forward she rested her hand over his chest and felt the pounding of his heart even as he moaned. When her tongue passed over his pulse Megan's need leapt forward, but she wanted him to enjoy himself as much as she was.

Megan ran her fangs along the pulse, not breaking the skin but close enough to leave her mark. Nuzzling her nose behind his ear she nipped none too gently at his lobe and lapped up the tiny drop of blood there.

"*Ne me taquiner ou je ne serai pas capable d'attendre. Maintenant.*" He yanked her away from his neck, his fist tight in her hair. "Take me now, Megan. Take me now or I won't be able to be responsible."

He pressed her back to his neck again and before she could think about her actions, she bit him. Beau's hot, rich blood filled her mouth. His heart was pumping so hard she didn't need to suckle to draw him in, he flooded her mouth. His hand at her head and the one at her hip held her to him as she drank with greed. It kept her in place as she took her fill. When she started to pull away, his sharp "no" kept her to him; his hips rocking up to meet her had her groaning.

His free hand traced her thigh and then around to her front. He cupped her mound and had her surging into his fingers as they dug into her, pressing against the fabric of her pants and into her clit.

"Come," he demanded against her mouth. "Come now to take the edge off of us both."

Megan didn't need to be told twice.

The climax ripped from her. Her body bowed on his, breasts pressed hard to his muscled chest. Even as she came down her body still rippling from the explosion, he pressed against her a second time, then a third. His harsh, "again" had her screaming out his name as her body did as he bid. When his fangs slid into her wrist she came again, a short blast of pleasure that had her nearly cross-eyed. While not as sharp, it was no less potent.

When he sealed the small wound at her wrist, she did the same to his. Licking the small pinpricks she leaned her forehead to his.

"We are home. When we get into the house I will be hard pressed to be civil to anyone thanks to you. I need you, Megan. My cock deep in your heat is what I will be as soon as I can possibly manage it. If you do not wish me to take you on the floor, or even in this limo, you will need to get quickly to our lair."

A shiver of pleasure ran up her spine. She didn't try to figure out how a body that just had three incredible climaxes could be ready for more, but she was. His growl made her giggle. He picked her up and sat her beside him on the seat. Still laughing, she opened the door and slid out. Beau was already in front of her.

"Hurry. Do not speak to the household, do not dally at all or the others will get a show that would only serve to embarrass you and satisfy me."

Still grinning she went into the house. But it wasn't her fault, she thought later, that she didn't make it to the lair right away. It was the couple sitting in the parlor with Duncan serving them. And Duncan looked less than happy about it.

"Mom? Dad? What are you doing here?"

~~~

Beau looked to the couple on the settee. He would never have guessed that they were her parents and with a quick sniff of the air around them he realized that they weren't. Looking at Megan he could see that she knew it as well. Beau looked over at Duncan.

"The master has been informed of the…visit. He is on his way with my lady. She is not very happy, my lord."

Beau would just bet she wasn't. Sara would probably tell these two if he knew her well enough. Beau took Megan's hand and pulled her to him. He wanted it known right from the start that she belonged to him.

"We came when…that man told us you were…we've been worried about you, Meggie. We were very worried when you didn't come home for so long. He wanted us to…we wanted to see how you were doing," the man stuttered.

Something wasn't right. They were terrified. Not of Megan, he was sure, but of someone. Beau wondered if it was the beast. Then he realized that it couldn't be. He didn't know Megan's name.

"I'm sure that the master of this house will be here shortly. In his stead, I would have you have a seat and let me see to some refreshments. Megan, please, I will return momentarily."

Beau left the room just behind Duncan. Beau was sure that the man seldom, if ever, had a show of temper, but he had one now. He was practically vibrating from it. When the kitchen door closed behind them, Duncan growled deep in his throat and had the older woman standing there raise a brow at him.

"Is Aaron on his way here?" Beau nodded to the woman. "Could you please see to some refreshments for the people in the living room?" At her nod, he turned back to Duncan.

"They just came into the house as huge as you please, Master Beau. When I tried to tell them…oh thank you, sire." Duncan drank the bourbon straight down without so much as s grimace. When he handed the tumbler back to Beau he automatically refilled it. Duncan continued after a sip this time. "When I tried to tell them that the master was not in residence they told me that they would wait in the sitting room. We do not have a sitting room, Master Beau. Whatever shall I do with them?"

Beau smiled. He'd heard about Duncan's childlike literal stance on things. He was sure that the man was a little too nervous and mad to correct now.

"We will entertain them until Aaron comes back. I'm sure that if you call him…" At Penny the cook's nod, he continued. "He'll be here very soon. I'm sure that he can figure out what to do with them."

He hoped. After making sure that they were both going to gather up some refreshments, or whatever it was that humans expected in this day and age, he went back to the living room. It appeared that no one had moved and Megan was in a fine snit.

She glared at him when he closed the door behind him and she stood up. Beau was on his guard. He didn't want her to get hurt, nor did he want to have to explain to Aaron why humans had seen him get hurt.

"I'm going to bed. I don't know why you're here, nor frankly do I care. You lied to me and I—"

"We didn't lie to you, young lady, and don't take that tone with me. You are still my daughter and I can still spank you—"

Beau didn't mean to growl at Megan's dad, but it was out before he could stop it. The man needed to back off and Beau wasn't sure that this was a good idea. They were all volatile and he, for one, didn't want to deal with it. He heard Duncan come into the room and nearly sighed with relief. Until he got a look at what he was serving the couple.

"Duncan, I don't think—"

"When people who are uninvited come into the master's house they cannot expect to get the best we have to offer. Though I do believe that the master has good taste in his beverages." When Duncan winked at Megan Beau nearly swallowed his tongue. "Here you are, Mrs. Reed. I believe this is wolf. I have some nice Fae if that would suit you better."

When the woman looked at the wine glass full of blood her face paled to near the color of fresh snow. She looked at Duncan then at her husband and shuddered before she set the glass and its contents on the table in front of her and stood. "I told you this was a bad idea. I told you that she was a bloodsucker now and would only be worse than she was as a child. Now would you please take me from this...this place and take me home?" She looked at Megan. "I loved you as a child. You were placed with us to raise as our own. But never, not once, did he say that you'd become a...you would become a monster. My heavens, you drink blood from dead people. How could you?"

Megan stood and so did Beau. He didn't touch her; the anger boiling off her was hot and menacing and he was afraid it would burn him. He watched as she took a step forward, then another. When she took a fourth then a fifth she was standing before the older couple.

Opening her mouth wide Beau could see her fangs. He was sure that the people not a foot from her had a much better view of their size and potential danger. A quick look at Duncan had him smile. Duncan looked like a proud papa as he stared at Megan.

When she leaned over and picked up the glass her "mother" had set down, she put it to her nose and inhaled deeply. Then, without taking a breath, she put the glass to her mouth and drank it down. With a swipe of her hand across her mouth she set the glass down again. "Hummm, virginal wolf blood. Nothing like it. You should have a glass. Perhaps it will loosen you up a bit."

Mrs. Reed swayed and had it not been for her husband she would have hit the floor. Beau was trying his best not to laugh, but there just seemed to be no hope for it. He felt it burble out of his mouth then turn into a full belly laugh as the couple started to race from the room. They stopped dead in their tracks and everyone turned to the doorway. The master of the house was home, it seemed, and he wasn't any happier than Duncan had been.

"Good evening. Welcome to my lair. Would you like to stay for a...bite?"

Mrs. Reed did faint then and it was everything Mr. Reed could do to get her out of the room with him. Beau was sure that the gate was already open and that Duncan was right now making sure they were gone.

"Well," Sara said as she sat down and put her feet up. "That was lovely. Megan, darling, do you think you could get me a glass of that fine virginal wolf blood? I find myself quite parched."

Chapter 18

Aaron watched Megan pace. He let her knowing that she had to work whatever residual anger off or explode. He looked over at Beau and realized that he had it bad. The man was head over heels in love with the girl and he didn't seem to grasp that yet. Time, Aaron thought, time would tell. He looked back at Megan as she turned to him again.

"They said they loved me. How is that possible if, at the first sign of trouble, they run like I was trying to drain them?" She took another turn on the carpet. "And how did you know what would scare the pants off her?"

Aaron didn't bother answering her. She wasn't really looking for answers so much as she was venting. He watched as she began to walk harder. Beau looked lost; Aaron knew that feeling. Women, especially strong-willed ones, were a unique breed. He didn't know what he'd do without his Sara and knew that Beau, even though he didn't realize it yet, would feel the same soon enough.

She stopped suddenly and Aaron wondered if what they had said, or actually what they hadn't said, had occurred to her. He thought it had the moment she turned and looked at him and Sara. Beau stood and waited too.

"She said 'he' had told her to come to me. She said that he, not them, not her, but he. What does that mean?"

Aaron didn't move. He'd been waiting for this. He'd been in both the humans' minds. It wasn't that hard; they were easy to invade and he had done so. He knew a great deal about the woman in front of him.

"As you have surmised, they aren't your parents. They aren't even any relation at all to you. You were right about the wolf. The female that came around when you were small was your biological mother. She is dead, by the way. But they don't know how or why. I'm sorry about that, Megan."

She waved him off. "How can I be the kid of a wolf? I'm not wolf. I'm not even human anymore."

"No, you're not human, but you are part wolf, or so they've been told. Since you've been staying here I've not been able to get a read on you. Sara has. She knows a bit more about you than me."

"Sit down, Megan, please. I'm so tired and cranky with this baby I don't think I can watch you pace anymore." Megan did what Sara asked. "You are part wolf mostly, I would suppose would be a better term. Your father was part as well, but your mother was full. Her brother, Michael, placed you with the Reeds when you were a baby."

"So, he's the 'he' they were talking about? This uncle of mine sent them here to do what? Spy on me? Kill me? I doubt very much it was supposed to happen the way that it did." Megan sat down only to bounce back up again. "And do you believe they thought we were telling them the truth about the blood? Oh please. How stupid do you have to be to think we can tell what kind of blood it was and whether or not it was virginal?"

Aaron shifted in his chair. He wasn't sure how to answer that one, but was saved from doing so when Beau stood again.

"We do know. You should as well. Know it's wolf and if it's a virgin. It's what keeps you safe, keeps you from drinking blood from someone tainted with black magic or a woman who is pregnant." Megan looked over at Sara as Beau continued. "Her blood wouldn't poison you, it wouldn't even make you sick…well, hers might. But as part of our DNA we neither drink from the young nor the pregnant."

Megan stared at Sara. Aaron could almost see her mind at work. She was shrewd, Aaron would give her that. And she was smart too.

"I smell nothing, nothing at all on you. I can smell him." Megan pointed at Aaron. "But nothing else on you. Why is that?"

Aaron had wondered the same thing. "When I first met you the night that you saved the little cub I could touch your mind. And since I have taken your blood I should have a connection to you that can't be broken. But I don't have that, not anymore. You are as lost to me as if we had never met."

Megan started to pace, but stopped suddenly and went to Sara. Gently she reached out her hand and reverently laid it on their unborn child. Aaron stopped Beau with a simple lifting of his hand. Aaron wasn't worried about Megan hurting his mate or the child. He wanted more than anything to see what she would do.

"It's a boy. He's…he's happy. I can feel his happiness. He told me that you talk to him, both of you and his brother and sister…he thanked me for saving Mac." Megan looked at him. "You told him, he said, while his mother slept, you told him how I had saved his brother."

"Yes. He has a right to know that you are a part of our family now. He needs to know you saved Mac, his brother, from certain death. And you are, Megan, a large part of my family, my kiss."

Megan moved away from Sara. "I'm tired. I can feel the sun coming up. I should…I have to go now. I have a lot to think about and some things I have to decide on." With a quick nod Megan left Beau standing there looking after her.

"A man came to visit me today. Not physically, but mentally. He told me that he would speak to me in my dreams, that he would tell me what I needed to know." Beau turned and looked at first Sara then Aaron. "He said that I can't tell the beast what her name was and that I was to protect her at all costs. Then he changed."

Aaron felt the room tighten with a surge of magic as Mel, the queen, and her father and grandfather shimmered into the room. They looked to Aaron like they had been up for days; their usual calmness now looked back with untold stress.

"Michael came to you in a dream because he knows that you'll help her. He can no longer protect her. He's hoping you will," Mel explained with a catch in her voice.

"Mel and I have been over the records of birth. We've traced down what may have happened to young Michael and who he is with now. But the monster he has become, he needs to be destroyed." James had his books as he spoke and Phillip had some charts he began to spread out on the tables. "We've narrowed it down to four men, all vampires and all with considerable powers."

Aaron stood and watched Beau leave the room. He would fill the young vamp in later. He knew that he had to see to his mate.

~~~

Beau found her in their room. She had locked the bathroom door, but that wouldn't keep him out if he wanted in. He knocked on the door gently, hoping Megan would let him in.

"I'm thinking. Don't you have something to do? Drain a young virgin or something? I'm kinda busy in here and I'd like some quiet time."

Beau grinned. "No, no virgins tonight. I'd like to talk to you, Megan. We have to talk about what happened tonight with your parents."

"They aren't my parents, you idiot. Don't you pay attention? They aren't my parents and they hate me." He pressed his hand against the lock and unlatched it from his side. "What do you think you're doing?"

"Talking to you without a door between us. And I doubt anyone could hate you after they get to know you. They were scared, that's all. You aren't the little girl they raised."

Megan was sitting in the tub with her back to him. He didn't mind the view from this end and sat down on the floor with his back against the counter. Every time she raised her legs or moved her arms, it was like a sensual moving art with muscle and skin.

"No shit, Sherlock. I'm a monster. And now a monster is coming here to get me. How wonderful." She raised her leg again and ran the sponge down it; water streamed along it in sparkling rivulets.

Beau lifted his hand and several candles that had been placed around the room lit. Then he turned the light off without getting up. The room was bathed in sensual light and soft scents, the smell of her soap and the candles mingling together to make his mouth water. He doubted that Megan had any idea what picture she was painting for him.

"Nice trick." She lay there for several minutes without speaking. Beau wasn't worried. He knew she had to work out whatever it was she wanted to say. When she did he found himself hurting for all that she had lost.

"When I woke up that first night I didn't have a clue where I was or what had happened to me. When Alfred bit me he kept telling me he was hungry and that he was sorry. He hurt me. He bit me so hard and so deep that I hurt for days afterwards. Is it supposed to be like that?"

"No. You know when I bite you it doesn't hurt like that. There is more pleasure than pain when we bite, isn't there?" He held his breath waiting for her to answer.

"Yes. No. I don't know. It's not painful when you do it, but…I don't know what you feel. I know that men get…they like it when I bite them." He couldn't stop the growl and wasn't even sure he wanted to. "Don't be all stupid on me. I had to eat and it creeped me out when I drank from women."

"There will be no more men or women for you. You'll only be able to drink from me anyway." She giggled and he sat back again. "What were you told about being a vampire, Megan?"

She lifted her leg again and wiggled her toes. Beau thought it was the most erotic thing he'd ever seen. When she lifted her other leg he had to adjust himself or he was going to hurt.

"Nothing. I didn't know what to do, but I figured out quick enough that the sun was painful. Then I would get so tired during the day. It was as if I couldn't keep my eyes open at all. I went to the library to see if I could figure out something, anything, but all I got was stupid stories about Dracula and some silly stories about how much fun it was to become a vampire. It's not fun, nor is it anything I would recommend to anyone."

"The sun will pull at you less and less as you age. After a few decades you'll be able to withstand more of it, but never full sunlight. Aaron can, but he is very old and he has Sara to help him with her magic." He thought about his turning. "Your maker, he was supposed to tell you everything you needed to know to survive, but he didn't seem all that much older than you in terms of being a vampire."

"No. Alfred had only been missing for about two weeks when he approached me in the parking lot. And until then he was a doctor like me. We were both waiting on our boards to come back." She turned to him then. "I don't want to hurt anyone. Ever. If there's some rule that I have to change some people to live, then somebody might as well kill me now."

Beau stood up and gathered her out of the tub. She soaked him and the floor, but he needed to hold her more than anything. He sat on the toilet with her and started to dry her off with the towel on the counter.

"There are rules about changing humans to vampires. A vampire can change his mate if she is willing, or not if she chooses not to. She will still live a full and long life, but she will die if she is hurt. A vampire can make a person a servant, someone that they trust to watch over them during the light hours, and they too will live for a long, long time." Beau stood her up and wrapped the towel around her body then picked her up.

"Like Mr. Duncan. I guess he's been around for awhile too. How old is Dingdong anyway?"

Beau laughed. "Aaron is fourteen hundred years old. Mel, the queen, is ageless. I think I heard Kyle say that she is older than time. I'm over four hundred years old, a mere baby in the scheme of things."

He put her on the bed and tucked her in. When he was satisfied with the blankets he went to the other side and stripped down as she watched. He wanted her in the worst way, but he knew that she was exhausted too. The sun was high in the sky and he could feel its pull too.

"Tonight you are not to leave our bed. I plan to make love to you very thoroughly, *mon amour*. Then, when I have had my fill of you, I plan to do it again." He slid into the bed. "Now sleep. You will need your strength."

When Megan rolled over and wrapped her body around his he sighed. She felt good there, almost as if she had been doing it for centuries. He wrapped his arm around her waist and pulled her naked body over his. Beau didn't think he'd be able to sleep with her nakedness over him, but he was out in no time.

Chapter 19

Michael knew the moment that Beau fell asleep. He knew the man had his mate close and was pleased by that. Very gently he moved into her mind, careful not to leave anything of himself or the beast behind.

She was brilliant. Even in her restful sleep her mind was working on problems, issues. He even found her working on a math problem, running the figures in neat columns in her mind as though it were a sheet of paper. Michael was happy to see that when she did get her part of him she would not be hurt by it. Moving out he did give her a little of his magic, just a bit to keep her safe, to keep her from being too overwhelmed with everything. Next, he moved into the mate's mind.

Beau was more complex. He was just as brilliant, not as much as the girl, but he was a fast learner. Michael was glad for that; he would need to be in the coming days. He hated to wake him, but time was running short and Michael needed to talk to him before the beast woke again.

"You are very lucky, you know," Michael started out with. *"Your mate, she loves you very much. Some days she wants to bash your brains in, but she does love you."*

Beau came to him slowly, the sun and the time of day beating at him. Michael gave him a bit of magic too, just enough to help him wake and stay that way more so in the day.

135

"You said you'd come. I didn't...I thought perhaps that I had dreamed you and that you were not real."

"I am real enough." Or, Michael thought, *real as I can be like I am.* *"We do not have a great deal of time so you must listen. The beast that comes for her, you understand who he is now?"*

"Yes, well, no. He's you, but I don't understand how that is possible. How can you be two different people like that?" He could feel the man's struggle with it and wished that he had more time to explain.

"I am us both but not. The beast, he is the part of me that is evil. More than evil, he is all evil. I didn't mean to create him. I only meant to bring out what I thought was the best in me, the part of me that would make me stronger, more aggressive. I got too greedy. I went too far." Michael wished daily that he'd had the strength in those first days to have ended his life. Now he had no control over any of it. The beast and the man, the one who caged them, controlled them now.

"There is a man, a vampire, that has us in his power. I'm not sure what he has, but he can keep the beast and me in turn in his dungeon. You must find him and destroy him as soon as the beast is destroyed. He has been working on a way to make more of the magic that made the beast. I cannot...I'm not strong enough to hide the information from the beast and he shares it with the vampire."

"Is the other, he calls himself Creature, is he...can he be killed? And what happens to you if he is killed? Do you die as well?"

Michael could be impressed if he was sure the man would do what he asked if he knew the truth. Michael was attached to the beast, attached to him because they were one.

"I will have peace from him. But you cannot destroy the beast, mon ami. Your mate must do that. When she does then she will be able to destroy the vampire and all those that come after him. The magic that holds the beast, within it is the ability to destroy the power."

136

Michael could feel the beast pulling at him, waking from the sleep that Michael put him in to rest himself. He was getting stronger and soon, Michael thought, very soon, he wouldn't have any rest.

"She isn't very old. Her…my mate, she doesn't even know what she is capable of yet. How will she destroy the beast when she can't even do the things her kind can do? I can't let her be hurt. She is my responsibility to care for, to protect. I don't think I can allow her to do what you need."

Michael had forgotten about the vampire code. He knew that the young vampire wasn't just saying that; he couldn't. Vampire males protected their mates above all else, including themselves. The beast stretched in his skin, making Michael aware that time was nearly out. He had an idea and decided that this was the only way.

"I will give you what she needs. It's the only way. When she gets it from you, she will know. It will help her to understand, help her with…everything. We must hurry; the beast, he wakes now." Michael didn't wait for the vampire to give his consent or not, he just pressed it hard into his body. He could feel the jolt of it hit him. The man would be hurting soon if he wasn't already. Michael jerked from the vampire's head just as the beast took him over.

The beast took him. Michael fought to stay aware. He tried to keep his own mind merged tightly with the beast and was surprised when the shift finished that he was there too. Once he saw where they were headed Michael wanted to hide away again, but knew that, if nothing else, this would give the young couple an advantage they would desperately need.

"You think to kill Creature? You are weak man, weak and useless. I am Creature, I am strong. To destroy me would destroy all."

Michael didn't answer. He had told the vampire the truth. He would have peace. Michael needed that, craved that more than anything.

When they made it to the mansion Michael looked around. He could see the same things the beast did, but Michael would retain them, analyze them for use. The beast only saw the fence that blocked his way in, not the way to get through it. And Michael was good at figuring things out. He smiled to himself. Yes, he was very good at figuring things out. Exhausted at trying to stay alert with the beast soon took its toll. Michael pushed the information to the young vampire and fell away, hoping that he didn't give anything away in his haste.

~~~

Megan woke on a scream. A climax ripped through her body and was charging up for another when she looked down at the man between her legs. Beau was taking full advantage of her nudity.

"You owe me, *mon amour*. You had three releases in the car and I got nothing. I even had to sleep with your beautiful body draped over me all night while my cock ached for release. You will now pay for that."

She wasn't sure she would consider this punishment, but yeah, if he thought so who was she to argue? When his fingers slid into her, she arched up and into his mouth. Beau had a very clever mouth and she wanted more. When she started to reach down and dig her fingers into his hair she realized she was tied to the headboard.

"Beau? I can't touch you. Untie me, please."

He looked up at her, his chin and mouth covered in her juices. It was incredibly erotic to see him like that, her thighs over his shoulders. She moaned and closed her eyes even as she rode his hand.

"*Je ne pense pas ainsi*. No, I think you will enjoy this more tied up. You distract me when you have your hands free. I mean to have my fill of you first."

His mouth covered her again. His hand under her ass tilted her up and he dove deeper, his tongue and his fingers filling her. Megan pulled at the restraints and thought about them holding her back, keeping her from touching him and her body loved it.

When Beau slid his finger into her tight hole she rose up off the bed and tried to get away from the invasion, but he kept pressing until the burn of him entering her had her cry out. Not from pain, but from incredible pleasure.

"Relax. I will not hurt you." In and out of her, he stretched her. "Feel the pain turn to pleasure, love? Do you feel the way I fill you here?" His finger hit a spot in her ass that had her moaning. "And here?" The finger in her pussy did the same, touching a nerve that set her body to flame.

Megan couldn't stop, she wanted them both. When he inserted another finger and the burn again turned to heat then pleasure she couldn't seem to get enough. When Beau worried her clit with his tongue then began to lap at his fingers she could feel her body rising to another wave. She wanted to look away, the overwhelming sensations making her dizzy, but to watch him enjoy her, suckle at her, was too much. When her release hit her, it was as if her body exploded; every nerve, every fiber of her being tightened like a rubber band before it snapped her breathless. When she came she screamed until she was hoarse, her throat raw with it, her body taut with it.

Even as she was shuddering with the aftermath, the delicious sated feelings, Beau crawled up her body and slammed into her. His cock filled her. She felt another climax building. This one she knew would kill her. When her hands were suddenly free she grabbed onto Beau, digging her nails deep into his shoulders as she wrapped her legs around him and held on. With each pound of his cock she felt it, felt him touch her womb.

Megan wanted to bite, needed to taste him as he filled her. Wrapping her fingers in his hair she brought him down to her, his head tilted so that she could lick his pounding pulse. He pulled away and looked down, his eyes dark with his need, his fangs nearly an inch long, sharp and lethal.

"My heart, feed from my heart, *mon amour*. I will take from your neck. I would taste your hot blood there."

Megan wanted him too, she realized. Never had she thought that she'd let anyone bite her neck again, but she gave him her throat. When she felt his tongue slide hotly along her neck, Megan came. Then when his fangs bit, she came again, her body coming apart and shattering.

When he sealed the wound Megan sank her own fangs deep into his chest and he roared above her his cum filled her, heated her. His blood poured into her mouth and slid down her throat. It seared her, the spice of it different and stronger there. As another climax ripped from her she drank more until she felt him drop onto her. Sealing the wounds she rolled with him as he moved.

The pain, horrific pain, had her opening her eyes and leaping from the bed. Grabbing her head, Megan screamed. Her head felt like it was ready to explode or implode, she wasn't sure. Wishing for both or either, she tried to get away from the hands, Beau's she thought dimly, but it didn't matter. Anything, everything was too much.

The blood on her hands told her she was bleeding somewhere; the pool of it in her lap told her it was her head. Her eyes felt too large and as if they were going to explode. Her ears rang and needles felt as though they were being inserted from the inside out. Her mouth stretched, her fangs dropped. Something banded around her and held her. Fighting it seemed too much when every part of her was in pain. Megan tore at her head, at her neck, and at her belly. Then she was sick, her belly rebelling harder than it had when she'd been turned.

It was impossible to scream again. Her throat was raw. Her head, she was sure, had fallen off and was now in the fireplace roasting like a marshmallow on a stick. She felt her muscles pull, lengthen, and hurt. Not even her nose was spared of torture as it felt like she'd inhaled a whole lemon into it.

After what Megan was sure was several days the pain lessened. After a bit longer she could take a breath without a searing pain. Her head began to feel normal and her body her own.

As it lessened, she became aware of things. The arms banded around her were Beau's and the man at her feet was Aaron. There were others in the room, many she knew, one or two that she didn't. Weak now, she couldn't do anything more than just lay where she was. Not even the soaking blanket around her was uncomfortable enough to make her ask that it be removed. The voices in the room seemed to be loud, but when she thought about asking them to lower their voices, they did. She wondered if she had spoken out loud. Megan closed her eyes.

After awhile she felt the blanket being removed and another put in its place. This one was soft and dry. She knew it was cotton without looking. She must have dozed because she soon felt the bed beneath her; more blankets lay over top of her. Weak as a kitten she kept her eyes closed even when someone, Beau, kissed her on the mouth. She didn't stir, didn't move, but lay there. Megan wanted to ask what had happened, but it was too much, too overwhelming. Soon, very soon, she was asleep.

Chapter 20

Beau had never been more terrified in his life. He watched Megan sleep and wondered again what had happened. He thought that if the man, Michael, had done this to her Beau would tear him limb from limb. He had hurt his mate.

Beau had been nearly asleep when she woke up jumping from the bed. He thought she had been going to jump on him when she screamed the first time. Beau tried to grab her, to hold her, but she fought like a madwoman. Her nails, claws really, had torn at him, at his skin and his face. He had had to leave her for a minute to go to the door and let Aaron in. It was by far the hardest thing he'd ever done in his life. Aaron had felt her pain too, her blood making them both aware of everything that happened to her.

When she started to fight them both and was succeeding at throwing them off Sara had come into the room and put her into a magical brace, banding her down so that she wouldn't hurt herself or anyone else. That too proved to be nearly not enough. Megan fought it as if it were nothing more than the silken ties he'd tied her to the bed with.

Beau felt Aaron return to the room a few minutes later. He was going to have to explain what had happened to his mate and Beau wasn't even sure himself. Aaron sat down in the chair on the opposite side of the bed from Beau.

"Mac is on his way home. Thomas said that in a few days he'll be as good as new. I'm sure that Lizzy will complain about him, but she'll be happy for it too. She's never been separated from him before. I have a hard time remembering that they are almost eleven years old. It seems like only yesterday they were born."

Beau looked up at the master. "I will pledge to you as soon as you are free. You...she is...I'm in love with her."

"Yes, I know. It's hard when they hurt. Harder still when you can't fix it." Beau nodded at the man. "I take it that you know what happened here tonight."

Beau nodded again. "Michael told me that he was giving me something for her. I thought...I'm not sure what I thought, but I assumed it would come in a box, not my blood." Beau was sure that's what had happened. He felt a connection to her now that he hadn't before. And he could feel she was stronger, more aware even in her weakened state.

"Whatever happened to her has made her different, more...more everything. When she wakes, do you know what she'll understand? What she'll know?"

Beau wondered the same thing. He looked up at Aaron again. The vamp probably knew, but Beau felt it was his obligation to tell him himself. "Whatever she is, I'm that too. I can feel my body humming with...with power. Incredible power, as a matter of fact, but not as strong as hers." Beau looked at Megan. "She fought off Sara's magic. I don't understand how she could do that."

Aaron stood and looked down at Megan. Beau could feel his need to knock the man away, but held back. For all his strength Beau wasn't stupid enough to think the man couldn't still rip his throat out.

"I won't hurt her. She is safe with me. I smell her wolf now and her magic. She's evolving, I think is the best way to put it. Evolving into what, I don't know. I've asked Sara to stay out until we can make sure she is no longer in pain. I can't have my own mate hurt." Beau understood. "When she wakes I would like to see her, speak to you both." Aaron went to the door, but turned before he walked out. "Bradley is upstairs. He's been made aware of her wolf status. He'll not claim her into his pack until he is sure of what she is."

"Thank you, sire." Aaron nodded at him. Beau stood near the bed now.

"Beau? She's going to be hungry when she rises. I'm sure you know that. Be careful. I know she won't hurt you, but we don't know what happened to her." With that, he left, closing the door behind him.

She would be hungry and have questions. Questions that Beau wasn't sure he had the answers for.

~~~

Megan woke suddenly. One second she was sleeping soundly, the next…crouched on the floor like an animal. Every part of her was in tune with everything around her. She could hear better, clearer; she could hear Mr. Duncan upstairs in the kitchen. Her sight was more focused, brighter, more colorful. Tones and hues leaped at her as she looked at things. Raising her face to the air she could smell bacon, eggs, toast with butter and grape jam. Megan could smell blood, not fresh, but from a wound, old but healing—Mac. She could smell Mac. She stood. The man in the bed confused her for a second the way he was looking at her, staring at her.

"Beau." He nodded, but didn't move anything else. "I'm different. I can feel you. You're in my mind."

"Can you speak to me this way, Megan? Can you touch my mind?" he whispered through his head.

"Yes," she answered back in the same way. *"I can feel you looking, searching. I'm all right. I feel…I feel wonderful."* She could feel his relief and smiled at him. "Something happened. The pain. Did I hurt you?"

He stood up and came toward her. Her body responded to his; she stretched and felt her body lean toward his. When he was close enough for her to touch Megan put her face in his neck and nuzzled. A low growl emanated from her mouth as she buried her nose in his throat.

"Megan, if you keep that up we're never leaving this room. The master...*merde*, you smell delicious."

His hands tightened around her waist and he kissed her head. Need coiled inside of her so tightly that she thought she might break from it. Licking the pulse that pounded there, she felt him shiver and marveled that something so simple could make him do that. When she nipped at his earlobe she found herself pressing closer to him. Then she stiffened and pulled back.

He stiffened and she knew that whatever it was that reached in her lust-filled mind he was feeling it too. Listening intently she searched for and found what had alerted her. Megan turned to Beau and smiled. "Sara is in labor. She is abusing her mate and telling him to call for me. He sounds like he is going to hurt someone. Should we go up?" She didn't wait for him to answer, but moved toward the door and then the stairs. She knew Beau was behind her as she could smell him. Things were starting to click into place; her mind a jumble of misinformation before, felt ordered and ready. It took her a few seconds only to realize that she knew how to shift, that her animal was a wolf. She also knew how to put someone into a compulsory state, to have them do just what she wanted them to do, needed them to do. Feeling confident for the first time in almost two years, Megan knocked on the bedroom door and stepped inside, Beau right behind her.

"About fucking time. I've been calling you for over an hour. Where the hell have you been?"

Megan grinned at Sara. The usual posh and polished woman sat on the edge of the bed covered in sweat and her hair looked like a rat had taken up residence. She had a blanket across her legs, but Megan could tell that she didn't have any pants on. Aaron looked terrified.

"Playing with my own mate. You're in labor and having fun too, aren't you? Well, let me see what you've been up to."

Aaron looked so grateful that Megan almost missed what Sara was saying.

"It never hurt at all before. Pete took it all away. I don't suppose you could do that, could you?"

"Nope. And even if I could, I'm not so sure I would. I think you might owe me. You've been butting into my life for a few days now." Megan helped Sara lay back. "When is the little guy actually due?"

"Last week. Just like his father," Sara threw a dismissive hand toward Aaron as she spoke. "He was being stubborn. I'm beginning to think all men are like that. Christ, I hurt."

Megan watched as Aaron paled more. She thought if he kept that up he'd be white as the sheets under his mate in no time. Taking pity on him she told the guys to step out while she examined Sara. Waiting through a contraction Megan knew it wasn't going to be much longer.

"Do you want Dingdong in here or not? We are about twenty minutes from lift off."

Sara glared, Megan grinned bigger. "You have to be more smart-alecky than Pete. She told me to brace myself, that she was going in. I had visions of her swooping inside of me and delivering my babies." After a few seconds of thought Sara shook her head. "I suppose she did. Is the baby all right?"

"Yeah. Ready to meet you, I guess. Don't know why. He's probably safer where he is. Not such a nice world out here."

Megan hadn't meant to say that. Her life was her own, but before Sara could comment another contraction ripped through the woman. Her scream for Aaron had him in the room and beside her in heartbeats.

It didn't take much time at all. Sara had told Megan between contractions that she'd been in labor since around noon, but had waited until dusk to tell anyone. "Not that anyone could do a whole hell of a lot anyway."

Baby boy MacManus, born at nine-seventeen that evening, weighed in at seven pounds and seven ounces; he was eighteen inches long. Once his bottom had a firm slap put to it Megan handed him off to his mother. While both parents held their child Megan finished up with the birth. By ten o'clock the bedroom was filled with people, mostly more vampires and other magical beings. Megan was slipping out the door when Aaron stopped her.

"You did a good job tonight, kid. Thanks. I owe you."

Embarrassed, Megan turned to the door and looked into the hall. "Yeah, I'll send you my bill. Listen, hum, do you think…I…well, I know this is a crappy time, but I need to tell you something. Something about what I've learned."

She felt rather than heard Beau come up behind her. She leaned into his strength when he slipped his arm around her waist. It was too calming to be here like this, but before she could pull away he pulled her into his body again.

"Of course." Aaron looked at his mate then back at Megan. "Now would be fine. Sara will be fine for a little while. Let's go to my office."

Megan wasn't aware that Beau had planned to be there until the lock set home on the door and he was inside with them. She looked at Aaron, but he was too busy sitting down…making a production of sitting she should have thought.

"He doesn't need to be here. If you think I'll jump your bones, you can—" She looked at Beau.

Aaron laughed. "He would try and hurt me if I were to be in a room with his mate without him, master or not. I'm sure you're aware that we vampires can be slightly possessive about our women."

Megan snorted. Like she cared. "He can stay or not. I could care less. I like him, but right now, this doesn't concern him."

"And he's right here," Beau said with a low voice. "If you do not wish for me to blister your bottom again, *mon amour*, then I would suggest that you get on with this meeting. We have unfinished business you and I." Then he whispered through her mind. *"I want you naked beneath me, me buried deep inside of you."*

When Aaron cleared his throat Megan turned to look at him. With narrowed eyes she swept his mind. He looked startled for a second, but didn't stop her from looking.

"You can't hear us. I don't understand. Why?" She sat in the chair across from his desk and waited.

"The path between mates is very private. The one between you and I is also private. It's the blood bond we have and the mate thing you and Beau have."

Megan looked at him. "You took my blood that first night. But you haven't…it's because I was blocked from you, right?" Aaron nodded. When Megan laughed he merely glared harder. "That must have burned your toast, huh? The Master Dingdong didn't have any control over something. I love it."

"Did you bring me in here to insult me or was there something important you had to say? And stop calling me Dingdong. My name is Aaron, or Master, but the Dingdong reference must stop."

Megan sobered. "I got…that pain was from Michael. I don't think he meant for me to have so much of him. He said it was to help me get a head start. I have it all, I think. He gave me a message too, about you. Michael said that you were to be trusted, that Mel trusted you so he would. The beast is coming here and he will use whatever means possible to get inside to get me." Megan got up to pace. "The beast is more than he had first thought he was. He's more powerful than he'd first imagined. He said that you should circle your wagons and call in the troops, that you're in for a showdown."

"So he wishes for you to stay here to fight him. Good, I have more men at my disposal that we could—"

"No. No one is to die for me." She put her hand up to stop both men from arguing with her. "He said that the beast, who calls himself Creature, by the way, will go through your men like paper. He said that only together, Beau and I can defeat him."

Chapter 21

"Then why did you tell Aaron that it didn't concern me?" Beau was pissed and he didn't care who knew it. "You thought to do this on your own anyway. And just how the hell were you going to keep me out of it, Megan? Hummm? Were you planning to sneak out of our bed to take care of it and slip back in like nothing had happened? *Merde*, you make me want to beat you at times."

"You try that, buster, and I'll make you hurt for a month, if not longer. You can't be hurt. It's...it's, I don't know why that's so important to me that you aren't hurt." She was shouting, but so was he.

When he realized that Aaron was laughing he turned on him. "This is not funny, *mon seigneur. Elle est ma vie. Si quelque chose devait lui arriver alors je—*" Aaron's raised his brow made Beau realize he was speaking French. "If anything were to happen to her then I would not wish to live, that is what I said."

"I understood. I just don't know why you're telling me and not her." Aaron sat in his chair. "But that is between the two of you. Now, Megan, tell me what we need to expect with the...Creature, did you call him?"

Megan looked at him and Beau was humbled by what he saw there. She was hurt and confused. When she turned away

Beau felt as if some part of him had soured, a part of him hurt because he had hurt her.

"Yes, he speaks of himself in the third person, for whatever reason. He is supposed to bring me back to a vampire." Megan stood next to the fireplace. "He's not sure who the man is, just that he is very powerful and very mean. Michael said that he cannot hope to win against him so long as Creature is in control."

"The vampire, as you know, is the one we met the other night. He is strong, though I believe that most of his strength comes from his confidence that the two men can defeat anything we put out there." Aaron reached for something on his desk. "His name is Samuel Rome. I've gotten some intel on him and it appears that he is approximately a thousand years old. He has a realm, though not large by any standards. There is plenty of money in the coffers and a few homes. He has just over a thousand subjects. According to the information Pete gathered he isn't well liked or respected."

Beau frowned. "Then what could he want Megan for? I mean a realm, money, subjects...Megan can't be his mate. What could she do for him?"

"Gee thanks. Your endorsement of my charms is amazing."

Beau flushed when he realized what he'd implied. "I only meant that with your temperament he can't think to keep you in line. You're not the most cooperative female I've run across." Beau looked over at Aaron who was having a coughing fit. "I do not understand. Am I not saying this correctly?"

"No, you're doing just fine if you're hoping to get yourself castrated," Megan snarled at him. "My charms notwithstanding, he doesn't want me for that. He wants my magic. Michael said that if he kills me himself all that I am goes to him. He plans to kill me to absorb what I am."

Aaron went to the door and opened it. Mel was standing on the other side. Aaron continued as she walked in. "What I don't understand is how he knew you had this magic. You didn't have it until tonight."

"She's always had it. Michael's been holding it for her, hiding it if you will." Mel sat down and a basket of fruit appeared in front of her. "My mate. He thinks I need more fiber. I'm going to fiber his ass when I get back to the castle. Anyway, your magic. According to my father's research you are a child of a female alpha wolf and a male sorcerer, Donald. Your mother changed him when he was still working for Rome as a chemist. When Rome realized what your mother brought to Donald as a mate he decided to bide his time and see what developed when they had a pup. Cybil, your mother, was also a healer and a mage in training. She protected you."

"Wait. Are you saying that my parents were fucking around with my DNA before I was born? For what, to make some sort of super baby wolf?"

"No. They didn't do anything other than love each other." Mel looked over at Aaron and, at his nod, continued. "Your Uncle Michael was away most of the time. He was experimenting with things that should have been left alone. When he discovered a serum that would prolong life without magic he used it on himself. Then before he could figure out what he'd done, he found out that his sister, your mother, was in trouble. He came to her aid immediately. But things went from bad to worse when he got there."

"And the end results? He used it without fully testing it, right?" Megan was pacing again. "But I still don't know what this has to do with me. Why does he think I'm this all-powerful thing that he needs to destroy?"

Mel looked at Beau then back at Megan. "He gave the serum to you. Well, he didn't give it to you, the beast did. He thought it would be a grand thing to have you as his mate. He would wait, you see, wait until you were old enough before he would claim you. The beast, not Michael."

Beau watched Megan as she absorbed this. At first she continued to pace then slowly turned to Mel when she stopped. When he started to stand to go to her Megan stopped him with a hand. Mel continued her tale.

"Your mother tried to save you. When she went up against the beast, he...he killed her. Michael burst through the beast and tried to save her, but it was too late. The beast and Michael fought for control and in doing so, you were injured too. Your father tried to save you with his magic and he did a good job too. But the damage was done. You had been marked, marked with a claw from the beast."

Beau has seen the scar. It was a long, jagged one that curved her right thigh. Megan rubbed it now and Beau was surprised that he could feel the burn of her touch as she touched her own skin. Mel looked at him when he glanced up.

"Michael gave you all that he was that night. The pain Megan felt was from the passing of his DNA, all of it in your mind then to your blood. I don't think he meant to give it all to you, but I will never be sure. That's what happened after Megan fed from you. The information and the knowledge that made Michael, all of him was poured into you." Mel laid her hand on Beau's head. "I can feel him in you, his thoughts, his dreams. That is what called me to you, or so I thought until I came into this house. It's Megan. She is Michael and all that he was."

"I don't want it. How can I...I wasn't even a person when I wasn't a monster, was I? All this time I've been a freak, a chemically enhanced freak that her parents couldn't even save." Megan started for the door, but she got no further than a foot before she stopped.

"You would do well to curb your tongue, Megan Allison Reed. I'm not a vampire that will tolerate you for the sake of humor." Mel's voice was low but full of strength. "Now, you will sit and another outburst like that and I will remove that flapping piece of skin you spout nonsense with." Beau couldn't rise. He tried and when Mel looked at him he calmed. "I'll not harm your mate as long as she listens. You'll sit there and be quiet or I'll send you to a realm so far away you'll be centuries getting back here. Now hush."

Beau was pissed. No one harmed his mate, no one. But the harder he fought against the bonds, the tighter they grew. Finally he gave up, but he wasn't going to forget this.

"We will deal with your lack of common sense at a later time. For now, you'll need to know what you can do. I can't help you other than to show you a few things you might need. Put out your hand, Megan Allison Desjardin." Beau could tell she was fighting Mel and was glad to know that it wasn't just him that Megan fought against.

"Fighting me will get you and your mate killed. Is that what you want? If so, then I'll just give you to Rome myself. Don't make your parents' sacrifice be for naught. Let me help you with this one thing."

Megan put out her hand. "Good. Now I want you to think about a weapon that you've seen before. You know which one I mean. Think about it."

"Weapon? I don't know what you mean. My par...the people I lived with didn't believe in—" Megan looked at Beau.

"Yes, that's the one. Think of it; bring it to your mind and think of all the details that went with it. All of them."

At first, there was nothing. Then Beau could feel a bit of magic, taste it as the seconds went by. Soon the room seemed to expand with it. He watched as Megan seemed to grow, rise from the floor, and then a bright circle went around her. Lifting her other hand Megan turned it toward him and he felt a strong pull toward her. Suddenly the bonds were gone and he was standing next to her, holding her hand and the magic surrounded them.

It took only a few minutes then the magic, the feel of it, seemed to dissipate. Soon it was nothing. When Beau leaned his head against Megan's she pushed him back and handed him a sword; a long, wide blade with a handle as wide as his own hand.

"It's mine. I found it one day when we were having a garage sale. I don't think I was supposed to find it, but I did. I had it hidden...I had hidden it away in the attic of our home. I couldn't even lift it then, I could hardly get it to where I'd hidden it without dragging it there. Now…" Megan swung the blade like she had been born to do it. "I know what I have to do."

~~~

Beau watched her. She wasn't sure what she was supposed to say to him, but he wanted something. Megan continued to practice with the sword as she thought about what the queen had told her, told them.

Megan's parents had been working at something that would make it so that some diseases could be eradicated. Cancer, for one, and a multitude of others that would make it so that the human race, the race they had tried to save, would no longer suffer as they did. Megan didn't know what to think and had said nothing. Mel had also given her a few pictures that she had of her parents.

"You do know that you can't do this without me, right?" Beau stood and came toward her.

"Yes. I know. You are the other half of me and without you…why?"

He looked at her strangely. "Why? Why what? What do you mean?"

She flushed. "Why do you want to help me? I understand that Michael gave you this information to pass on to me, but why do you want to help me? You don't really have to."

He took the sword from her hand and put it in the ground next to them. She looked up at him when he cupped her face in his hands. She swallowed hard. He looked so big standing there.

"Why. Well, I could say that I want to help because I want to see you kick some ass, but as you do that often enough to mine I don't think that'll be enough. I could say it's because you are my mate, but we both know that we can't live without the other and that's a poor excuse anyway. We do have this connection that bonds us and I don't mean the vampire one, but again that's a poor excuse."

She tried to pull away. He was making fun of her and she didn't need it. Not now and not later. If he didn't want to help then he should just say so.

"No, *mon amour*. I help you because I love you. With all my heart. You are not just my mate because the Fates have deemed it so. You are the mate of my heart. I love your laughter, though you do not do it near often enough. I love that you call our master Dingdong and he hates it, though I will never admit that to him." He kissed her mouth, a gentle brush of his lips over hers. "I love the way you make me feel, even in anger. I love the way you stand up to me; again, I will not admit that to anyone. You are my heart, my life, and my whole being."

Megan could feel the tears burn at her eyes. No one had ever said that to her before, not anyone. She leaned in to kiss him. A kiss as gentle as the one he'd given her and more.

"Oh, Beau. I love you too. I'm so glad you were a prick and made me be your mate." His burst of laughter made her flush. "I didn't mean that the way it sounded. I only meant that you had to force my hand."

"Yes, you did, but I don't care. It is just like you to be so honest that you would tell me that you love me and call me a prick in the same sentence."

The snarl ripped them apart and had them back to back looking for the sound. A shadow moved across their sight, but was gone in a flash. Megan peered deeper in the dark woods, but couldn't see anything. Before she could ask Beau if he did she felt him ripped from her side.

"Creature will kill him if you do not come with him. Creature wants to kill him, but will not if you come."

Mother fuck, Megan thought. The beast had come to play and now he had Beau.

Chapter 22

Megan stood her ground. She could tell that the beast, Creature, was near, but she couldn't see him. Her blade was drawn, but it was doing her little good if she couldn't see her enemy.

"Give me my mate and I'll go with you. Otherwise I don't trust that you won't hurt him. I'll go, but first, he comes out unharmed."

The laughter from all around her ran up her spine and made the hair on the back of her neck stand up. Eerie didn't cover it. Terror, horror, creepy…any and all of those including scared the shit right out of her didn't even come close to the feeling she got from the sound.

"Creature cannot give you unharmed mate. Too late for him to be unharmed. Too late, too late, too late." His sing-song voice echoed around the trees.

Megan felt the sweat trickle down her shoulders. "If he's dead then all—"

"Creature didn't say he dead, said he was not unharmed. Creature knows you aren't stupid. Listen. Listen to Creature."

"I'm not harmed too badly. Do not give up to him." Megan felt Beau whisper through her mind. *"I'll come back and kick your bottom if you do."*

Relief was profound, but she wasn't going to give him the satisfaction of letting him know how much it had affected her.

159

"You try it, buck-o, and I will...I will...you big jerk, what are you doing over there? I need you here, with me."

"Then perhaps you should do something about it. I am ready to come back to you, love. We have a conversation to finish."

She felt his humor and his pain. She wanted him near her. More than for his support magically, she needed him with her. Closing her eyes she could feel the beast moving along to her right. Beau was with him.

"It would help me if you'd get away from him first, you know. I have enough on my mind right now with all this love crap you're spouting." He laughed and she felt better.

"Creature is waiting. You will come to me, female, or Creature will kill the male." His voice was to her right, but she knew that he was more behind her. Then it occurred to her he didn't know her name.

"Michael? Are you there? Come to me, Michael. I want to see you."

The scream was a loud and piercing sound. Megan didn't believe it was from pain, but from anger. He was pissed about being called Michael. Good to know, she thought, and started to call out again.

"Creature will kill him. Kill him dead if you say that name again. No Michael, just Creature. Creature, Creature, Creature. I am Creature."

Anger makes the beast stupid. She didn't know where that thought came from, but it seemed to make sense. If he was pissed, he'd be reckless. If he was reckless then she could beat him. But first, she had to make sure that Beau was all right.

"Beau, I need to piss that thing off. I need to make him mad at me. Do you think I could do that?" She felt his humor and was warmed by it.

"I don't believe that should be a problem with you, love. You seem to have a knack for it. Would you mind terribly if you brought me to you again? Just want to be near you when you kill his fucker."

She wanted to be offended, but couldn't bring herself to be. She did have a knack for pissing people off, she knew this. Closing her eyes she thought of Beau; his hands, his face, and him being near her, his body, his warmth touching her. When she felt his hands move along her arm she opened her eyes again. She didn't expect to see the beast with him.

Megan grabbed for Beau the same second that the beast made a swipe at him with his claw. Beau dropped to the ground and she rolled over and came up behind the beast. Her blade came around in a full arc when he ducked and rolled forward. She had missed him. He stood and turned toward her and she got her first look at the beast.

He was abhorrent. She stepped back from him, not because of his size, which was enormous at over seven feet, but because he was…well, ugly. His skin was a patchwork of colors, blended and mashed together, browns and grays, hairy and smooth. His eyes were off center to his face, one a good two inches lower than the other and green while the other was a silvery pewter color. His lips were scabbed over in places and looked bloodied and sore. And instead of a mouth as a human might have, it looked as if he had a snout, a shorter version of a wolf or canine's. Not all of his teeth fit in his jaws and the ones that didn't slanted out and some even perpendicular to his face. They were long and short, sharp and flat, a mixture of the two of him mashed into one being. Cheek bones that were coarse-looking, broken that had not healed properly, gave him an obscene shape that made his skin stretch taut over them in places and hollowed out in others.

His shoulders were wide and muscled. He looked like a linebacker with pads on. His skin was scaled like that of a fish, each scale lapping over the other, giving him what appeared to be a protective shield. He was shirtless and Megan could see scars, deep ones that looked like they had been painful when they had been inflicted and smaller ones that looked fresh. His waist was small in proportion to his size, giving him an unbalanced look that only added to his overall appearance.

Along his massive arms the hair was coarse and wiry-looking, the muscles bunched and corded. His hands, though, his hands were terrifying.

His wrists ended at this forearms and his hands—and she only thought of them as hands because of where they were—were long razors in place of fingers. The blades, only three per hand, were about six inches long. Silvery in the moonlight, more deadly looking, she was sure, in the light of day. As he stood there he flexed them and Megan could see the blood on them.

"Creature thinks you're pretty, yes, Creature does. Come to me now, female. Creature will take you to Master and then we will play."

Megan felt Beau's body behind her. She didn't want the beast to remember him and moved to her right, away from Beau. She could feel his pain and was worried that he would be too weak to help her. She reached for him and was happy to find him still alive.

"You plan on taking a nap or getting up and helping me sometime soon? I can't keep carrying you, you know." She sent him warmth and love. *"If it's not too much trouble, that is."*

"I thought that a nap might be something perhaps we could both enjoy. You are to kill this beast, not I. I would not mind if you dispatched him sooner rather than later, mon amour.*"* Megan felt her world shift. *"I will be honest and tell you that I bleed still and hurt a great deal."* She wanted to go to him, but knew that if she did they would both be dead.

"I'm not going anywhere with you. You've been messing with the wrong girl if you think I'll just come with you quietly." She moved to her right as she spoke so that now Beau was behind the beast. "I like where I'm at just fine and dandy, thanks."

"Creature will have you. He will. And when Master is done Creature will have you more." He extended his claws and moved closer. "And if Creature does not, then no one will."

He lunged at her, his claw barely missing her throat. His laughter rang out and Megan felt chills race along her spine. He was playing with her. He was actually playing with her. Megan felt her anger surge and her body react to it. Before she could retaliate and lunge at him too, she felt a presence in her mind.

"He is strong but stupid. He is more but he is less. Think. Do not allow him to beat you at his own game."

"Michael?" Love washed over her, through her mind and her heart. His warmth touched her in ways that she'd never felt with anyone else. Not even with Beau. This love was different and she was strengthened by it.

Taking a deep breath she stood still. Her sudden stop seemed to confuse the beast. He stood still as well and watched her. Megan held out her hands, palms up and fingers wide. Her blade had been left in the ground, the point in the soft grasses. When her energy began to build she felt the blade hum even from where it was.

The creature growled and then started for her. Megan closed her eyes. Her body's energy began building and building; power washed over her and through her. When she opened her eyes again the beast was mere inches from her, his blades outstretched and sinking into her flesh. When his mouth opened, his breath on her neck, she felt the sword pommel fit into her hand, heard the sound of steel hitting flesh just as the beast closed his mouth around her neck.

~~~

Beau watched the beast attack his mate. He couldn't move to help her because of his wounds, couldn't take a breath for his terror. When the tip of the blade came through the beast's back then nearly a foot of it followed Beau tried to stand, his broken legs nearly healed but still weak. As he stumbled forward Megan took a step back, then another. The beast stood where he was.

Just as Beau stood up, the beast staggered back, his hand on his chest where the sword still embedded in him quivered from the impact. When he dropped to his knees he looked up at Megan and smiled.

163

"You cannot kill Creature. Creature is strong. Creature is big." His breath swished from his mouth. "You think to kill Creature when you can't. I am Creature."

Blood spat from his mouth. A long stream of it dripped from his jaws; the blood on his chest slowed as Beau watched. The beast fell forward onto his bracing hand and laughed out loud. He held himself up as he pulled the blade free. When it was out he dropped it on the ground and fell to his side then rolled to his back.

Then something started to change. He seemed to move. His body shifted and reshaped; his face aligned and became smooth. He appeared to shrink and remold himself. Soon, sooner than Beau would have believed, a man lay in his place, the man who was Creature. Michael had come through.

Michael turned his head and looked at them. Megan stepped forward, but Beau grabbed her before she could throw herself onto the man. He didn't trust that the beast wouldn't return, that he hadn't let Michael come through so that he could lure Megan to him.

"You are right to be wary." Michael's voice was soft. It held pain and wonder. "I cannot hold him for long. You know…you must do it, my child."

"I can't. You can't ask me to. Please. You have to fight him, please." Beau could feel her tears and her pain. He pulled her body to his and held her.

"I cannot. When he returns, I will no longer…there will no longer be me. He will win. Even now…he is regenerating… You look…my sister…you have the look of her. She would be so very proud of you." His coughing was getting stronger the blood all but stopped flowing from the wound in his chest. "You must do this for me. Give me peace."

Megan fought against his hold and for a second Beau wanted to let her go, but Michael's body rippled and shifted. It was slight, but enough to show that the beast was returning.

"Your name. I would have it before he kills all that I am." Michael's request sounded sorrowful and full of regret.

Megan turned to look at him. Beau wanted to tell her no, to tell her that he was dangerous with that information, but he could see her determination and knew that she had made a decision, the decision to do as Michael had asked. Beau nodded once.

"Megan Allison Desjardin. I love you. I will do as you asked."

Beau pulled Megan back as Michael closed his eyes. The smile on his face was serene and sad at the same time. Beau wanted Megan to remember the man this way, but the beast was returning. His shift was nearly complete when she leaned over and picked up the blade again.

"Creature is power. See? He returns. Creature cannot be killed, not by a female, not by his plaything."

While the beast was still forming he got to his knees. Megan gripped the sword and held it point down as the beast looked at her. Beau stepped back. He knew she could do this and she would. He had never been prouder of anyone in his life.

"You fucked with the wrong girl, buddy. Megan is strong. Megan is powerful. And this female is going to kill your ass."

Megan turned away, her back to the beast and her face set. She winked at him, blew him a kiss, and lifted the blade as she turned. Her body arching, the blade raising, she twisted around coming full circle. When she faced Beau again he started forward and stopped when she lifted her hand to him.

Turning back to the still kneeling beast she gripped the handle again, lifting it upward until it was in front of her face, the point to the sky, the pommel at her chin. Beau looked to the beast. She had missed.

Chapter 23

Megan looked at the beast as she held the blade aloft. As Beau moved behind her he gripped the blade and she laced his fingers with her own. When he pulled the sword, tried to take it from her, she stilled him.

"Wait."

The blood trailing down the body of the blade was at her level now; she could see it as it made its way from the top. When it was at the same level of her mouth she reached out and licked the stream off, taking it into her mouth and feeling the power of it surge through her. She knew the exact moment that Beau felt it as well; his fingers with hers on the pommel gave to him what she was.

She watched the beast now. None of them moved, not the beast, not Beau, nor herself. When a seam of blood appeared on the beast's throat she knew that her blade had rang true. As the seam grew wider more blood poured out until the beast reached up and touched his neck. When he raised his eyes to them he looked stunned.

Megan watched as the beast struggled for speech, his mouth opened but he couldn't form any words. Blood spilled from his lips as his tongue worked. Then his body went limp and dropped to the ground, crumpling into a heap. For several seconds his head was suspended there, seemingly floating in the air, and then it too dropped and rolled toward them. Megan stopped it with the toe of her shoe. The blank eyes stared back at her.

"Creature is no more. Creature is dead," she told it in a soft voice.

Before she could turn and be gathered in his arms Beau stiffened. Megan leaned back into his chest as the first wave washed over her. She knew that Beau was feeling it too. His body bowed with hers, his arms tight around her.

As the energy from the body in front of them left the creature it gathered at the tip of the blade still pointed skyward. As she lifted her head toward it the blue flame of it raced down the blood and slammed into her and, through her, into Beau. She cried out, and from what seemed like a great distance, she heard Beau do the same. It was over in seconds, she knew, but it felt like an eternity. Her last thought before she dropped to the ground was that they were going to be crispy critters if no one found them before daylight.

When she woke she was in a bed, the same she had been in before with Beau. Rising up, she saw him in a chair next to her. He was watching her, his face pale and taut.

"Are you awake this time? Or are you only looking at me? I'd like to see you again, *mon amour*."

She studied him then smiled when she realized that they were both alive. "I'm awake. Are you alright?"

Instead of answering her he stood up. When he crawled into the bed with her and pulled her close she realized that they were both naked and she felt as though she was safe. He held her so tight it was almost painful, but she wouldn't have it another way.

"You have been sleeping round the clock for three days. They told me that you had been through an ordeal that I need only wait, but I didn't believe them. You are…you are my heart, my life. Please, the next time that you plan to rest for so long, don't. I cannot stand it."

She laid her hand over his heart and felt it beat beneath her palm. "I'll remember that in case I have to kill a powerful beast again. In fact, next time, you can kill it and I'll wait for you. I'm probably better at waiting anyway."

He growled at her and she laughed. She wasn't sure she could have been any more patient than he had. Probably less so. He held her for a little while longer before he pulled back and looked down at her.

"Dr. Reilly said that the beast cut you deeply. I didn't know he'd hurt you until then. He said that you had lost a great deal of blood, or so he had thought, but he said that you didn't show the signs that would indicate that you had. I thought it was the power that we received, but I didn't say that to him."

Megan remembered the blood on the blade and that she had licked it off. She wasn't sure what had made her do that, but she'd known that she needed to. Then when the blue flame raced down it to her she knew that it was because of it that she was able to survive whatever had happened when the beast's and Michael's power came to her. She rolled over and sat up on Beau.

"You weren't hurt, were you? From the power, I mean. It didn't hurt you?" She searched his face, his arms, and chest. "He said that he harmed you. I know you were hurt, but how?"

"My legs, he broke them. But they healed quickly because of what we are." He pulled her to his chest. "*Mon amour*, we will need to find the vampire who held the beast. Michael told us that he is creating more of the serum to make more of the beast."

Megan shuddered. The beast, or Creature as he'd called himself. More of him out there would be a danger not only to others, but to humans as well. Looking up at Beau she thought about the fight ahead. "I don't want you hurt. I...I love you, Beau. I don't think I could bear it if anything happened to you." She kissed his chest over his heart. "I know that we will spend an eternity together and I want to get a start on that as soon as possible and just hide here."

He kissed her and she snuggled closer. If only it were that easy. They did have to go after Samuel Rome and soon. He would know by now that his beast was dead. Megan wondered if he knew who killed him as well. Probably. He would be after them soon if they didn't go to him and Megan didn't want the fight brought here. She sat up and looked down at Beau.

"We need to go. Soon. I don't know how long it will take him to get here, but he already has a three day head start." She started to rise, but stopped when Beau pulled her back.

"I wish to make love with you, *mon amour*. Now, before we leave this room." He pulled her over his body and sat up. "I would savor you this night, feed from you and you me. I need you, Megan Desjardin."

She couldn't speak. Her heart filled with love for him and she couldn't speak over the lump in her throat. Leaning in she kissed him; gently and softly, a brush across his mouth.

When he rolled her over and settled between her legs she wrapped her legs around his hips and her arms around his shoulders. Beau took her hands down, put them above her head, and held them there by lacing his fingers between hers. He looked into her eyes as he moved his body down hers then up again.

"You are wet, *oui*? I can smell your essences." His cock nudged at her entrance and she felt an answering rush of heat. "You heat pulls at me, begging me to enter you. Are you ready for me?"

She surged up to meet his cock. He slipped into her and then out again when he pulled back. She tried to move up to bring him into her again, but he pulled back.

"*Non*, I will savor you. We will go slowly this time. You are always in such a rush." He nipped at her chin and she surged up again.

She ached for him, all of him, and lifted her head enough to lick his throat. He rocked into her when she lay back.

"Please, Beau. I beg of you, please."

He slid into her again, then out again. It wasn't enough, not nearly enough. Wrapping her legs around him again, she pulled him to her when he rocked into her again and felt him fill her.

His groan rumbled along her chest from his. When he continued to rock deep she met his downward thrust with her own upward one. Soon they had a rhythm, slow and soft, in and out. Her body was building up; she could feel her climax coming onto her. But she wanted to feel him come first.

As his thrusts became more, filling her more, taking her more deeply, she licked his throat again. He tilted his head and nipped at her shoulder. He jerked in her when she ran her fang along the vein.

"Bite me, Megan. Take from me, bring me into you." He rocked harder, his timing off every time she licked his pulse.

She didn't bite him, didn't break the skin until he was pounding into her, his cock bumping her clit with every downward stroke. When he let go of her hands to pull her hips up to him she buried her fingers into his hair and pulled his head back, baring his throat for her. She struck quick and hard, her teeth sinking into his flesh hard enough to leave bruises. He bellowed out her name as he came. She was so mesmerized by his face, the beauty of it when he came, that she was surprised when her own climax gripped her. She threw back her head and screamed, her entire body seized in the moment.

As her body became her own, began to settle, he rocked into her slowly, bringing her to a softer and fulfilling climax. When she was cresting the wave this time he bit her. His fangs sank deep and brought her again.

~~~

Beau wasn't sure he'd ever be able to move again. His body was more relaxed, more sated than he'd ever been. He rolled to his back and brought Megan with him. She was limp and, had he not heard her heart beating, he would swear that he'd killed her. Chuckling a little he looked up at her when she raised her head.

"You are more than I ever dreamed of having in a mate, more than I ever wanted in one as well." She smacked him as he lay back. "You honor me by being my mate. I look forward to fighting with you for many centuries to come."

She snorted. He laughed. There would never be a dull moment with his mate and he would be very happy to tell Sara that she had been correct. He could not have been more wrong in what he wanted in Megan.

Neither said anything as they dressed. Megan had her back to him when he turned and saw the mark on her. A crest, he supposed. A double sword over a tree, the Tree of Life. When he moved closer to look at it he was surprised to see it move. He reached out and touched it and jerked his hand back when the tree moved under his fingers. He looked at Megan and she was looking at something behind him.

Turning to see the mirror behind him he could see the same marking. His was bigger, but it looked exactly the same.

They didn't speak, but they both began to dress quicker, needing to get to someone who might be able to answer what it was. Beau wasn't afraid, he wasn't even worried. He knew that whatever had happened in that field, this sigil was a part of it.

When they came above floors everyone was in the kitchen. Sara and Mel were seated at the table, a baby on each of their laps. Aaron and a man Beau didn't know sat there as well. The children, Lizzy and Mac, sat on the opposite side of the table eating what appeared to be a plate of cookies. Kyle and Maddie were there as well and Kyle pulled Beau into a hug, holding him tight for a long time. He even hugged Megan, who blushed bright red when Beau growled.

The alpha was there, as was his mate, also a woman Beau had met named Pete and another named Sam. Their mates were due to arrive soon. There was a large, dark cake on the counter and Duncan was cutting it into pieces and fussing over the crookedness of the cuts. Sara was telling him to just give her a slice or she would make him change the next poopy diaper.

"Megan, take the knife from him and cut me a slice of cake. I've not been allow to have chocolate for nearly nine months and I need a piece right now." Sara held out her empty but chocolate-smeared plate. "And I want a big one this time."

Megan took the knife from Duncan and with a wink at him, cut the smallest slice he'd ever seen of anything. Beau was sure one could read through it. They both laughed when Sara growled at them and got up and handed the baby to Megan. That shut her up immediately.

"That…this. I don't…what the hel…heck am I supposed to do with this? Here, take it back. I'll cut you some cake, just, I don't want this."

"Megan, I'm surprised at you," Aaron laughed. "You brought him into the world and you don't know how to hold him? That's not saying much for your bedside manner."

She handed him to Beau and backed away. "There's a big difference between delivering one and holding one when it's all babylike. I don't know crap about kids unless it's on the inside of them. I'll fix them when you break them, but I don't know anything else about them."

Everyone laughed and finally, after Sara was settled with her cake, she offered to take the baby back. Beau told her he didn't mind and held him as they talked. When the older children went to bed the adults went to the living room. There they started talking about the events of a few days ago.

"Rome is in my territory. He has permission so long as he behaves. He inquired about you, Megan. He wants to know when I plan to turn you over to him. I told him that you have pledged to me. He said that you owe him a child and wants to meet with you to see how you plan to pay him back." Aaron moved to the fireplace, taking something off the mantle. "He said that you left this at the ash site. Is it yours?"

Beau looked at the shirt. He could smell her on it, but the scent was faint. He took it from her when she offered.

"It's mine. I had it on the night…the night that Alfred…how did he get it? I left it in the caves when I was there."

Aaron nodded. "I thought so. I really don't know why he has it or thinks that it proves anything. And I don't know why he would think that you killed Alfred. A child cannot kill their maker. He should know this and let it go. But I will admit that I'm glad to know where he is."

Beau agreed. He liked having his friends close and his enemies closer. And Rome was an enemy. He looked over at Megan when she snuggled next to him. They had to tell them what had happened since coming back. But Mel beat them to it.

"You're both marked, aren't you? I can sense it because it's one of mine. The mark of the Royal Guard, or their crest. I'm assuming you got it from Michael. As his niece he would pass it on to you, Megan." Mel stood. "May I see it?"

Megan stood, as did Beau. Lifting his shirt and Megan pulling up her sleeve, they bared their marks to the queen. She started to touch them both, but looked at them first.

"You are a part of my guard if you wish it. It will give you more than you are now, but you'll have to leave this plane to be one. I want you to think about what I give you and decide if this is something that you both want. My guard is an elite group and answer to no one save the Fates. When I touch these marks you'll be able to come and go between the realms until you make the decision. Understand?"

"No. I don't. Are you saying that if we work for you, then this place, Earth, is off limits to us?" Megan looked at Beau then back at the queen. "No offense, lady, but I like it here just fine. I mean, I'll talk it over with Beau, but honestly I've worked too hard and waited too long to be a doctor and I'm thinking there isn't much call for one wherever it is you want us to go."

Beau pulled her into his arms. He couldn't agree more.

Mel laughed. "No, not any at all. And you will still be able to go between worlds. It is your right as one of the few. If you change your mind, you need only let me know." She sat back down and Beau moved to the couch and pulled Megan onto his lap.

Aaron cleared his throat. "We must discuss the master vampire Rome. He means to have you, Megan, and at any cost. What is it you plan to do about him? Or do you know?"

Beau kissed his mate and looked at Aaron. "Yes, we are going to kill his ass and take his realm."

Chapter 24

Aaron had hoped that was what he'd say, and when Megan agreed Aaron took his first deep breath in days. He'd been so worried about the two of them, more worried than he'd been about one of his kiss, or family, than he could ever remember.

He had plenty of vampires in his realm, a great deal of them female, but none as young as Megan. He liked the girl, even though there were times that he would gladly strangle her, but she had a good head on her shoulders and she had saved Mac. She had also brought his other son, Daniel Temple MacManus, into the world with little fuss. Aaron owed her and, in turn, her mate.

He knew from Kyle that Beau was a good man and had been a great leader among their kind. Kyle had told him that Beau had retired because he had been tired of his life and he feared that he would end it soon rather than hope for his mate. Aaron knew that a great many vampires gave up after searching for so long and knew that his own mate had saved him from the same thing.

Samuel Rome would die. And much sooner than Rome knew or thought. Aaron, for one, was glad for it. Aaron thought about the information that Pete had found on the man and realized then that Rome was slightly more evil than Carlos Sanchez, the man that Aaron had killed for the realm that he now ran.

Each man had a sadistic way about them, thinking nothing of murdering their own subjects in the name of justice. While Sanchez had been cruel to his subjects by starving them, Rome not only starved them, but also charged them for drinking from their mates. Pete had also found rumors that he killed any and all offspring of the mated couples, claiming that they were a drain on the already tight coffers. A search of those said coffers revealed that there was nearly one hundred million dollars in monies and land that the realm owned. Aaron would have been impressed if the whole thing didn't sicken him. He realized that he'd missed some of the conversation when his mate nudged him none too gently in the ribs.

"...meet him tomorrow night. I think that will give us enough time to get you all to safety. I won't have any of you hurt because I have an idiot on my ass."

Aaron grinned. "Beau, you going to let your mate talk about you like that? I mean come, man, an idiot on her ass?" Megan blushed again and Beau's sudden coughing fit had them all laughing. "You'll do well to remember, young lady, that I am master here not you."

"Listen Dingdong, we've gone over this before. I'll not have anyone die for me. Not before and certainly not now. You know that what I'm saying makes sense." Megan stood up. "I won't have it. I went to school for a long time to learn to save lives. Taking one was hard enough. Being responsible for as many as you have at your fingertips is just too many."

"Don't call me Dingdong." Aaron took a deep breath before he felt he could continue. "Megan, you are my subject and the sooner you realize that you answer to me and not the other way around, we should get along nicely." Aaron wanted to rethink his position on liking the girl when she turned to him again. He couldn't stand tears and was profoundly happy when there was anger instead of them. But she was going to push him too far. "Megan, you are—"

"Sire? There is a...person of questionable taste at the door. He claims that he has waited long enough. He would like you to turn over his property. I asked him what he meant and he said that he was here to collect Miss Megan. Sire, shall I show him what we do with infidels?"

Aaron looked over at Beau when he stood, pulling Megan up with him. "No, Mr. Duncan, I believe it will be my pleasure to show the man what I do with infidels. If you would be so—"

Aaron growled. He was tired of people assuming he wasn't in the room. "Sit!"

Everyone, including Duncan, sat. Aaron felt bad for that. Duncan didn't even try to sit in a chair, but had dropped where he was immediately.

"Now. We will do this my way. Beau, you and Megan will stay in this room and not say a word. Megan, I am serious, keep your mouth shut or I shall shut it for you. I think Beau will thank me for it." Aaron helped Duncan up from the floor. "Tell the man that I will see him on the morrow. If he doesn't like that, then tell him...never mind, just tell him tomorrow."

When Duncan left the room, Aaron turned to his mate. "Can you protect the house?" At her nod he turned to Kyle. "Call the warriors. Tell them that there is a vampire in the realm that means harm to Megan. Tell them I would consider it an honor if they were to keep an eye on him. Bradley, can you watch him during the daylight?"

Bradley nodded. "Consider it done. Do you want us to keep him safe or just watch?"

Aaron grinned. "For now, safe." When Megan stood Aaron turned to her. "If you plan to add to the conversation, fine, but if you spout any more nonsense about doing this on your own I'll not be responsible for what I do to you."

"You said Megan."

Aaron frowned.

"When you asked the warriors to come to your aid you said that they were being asked to protect me. Why should that matter? Why would they care about me?"

Aaron walked to her and touched her cheek. "Oh Megan, you are a quandary, aren't you? Tough as nails one breath, small child the next. They would be honored to watch over you because of what you have done for me and mine. When you saved my son you became someone they would die for. Not because I have said it, but because of what you did."

Bradley stood too. "And saving little JC from those men. We have since found the other men and they told us all about the children they had been taking all over the state. Dozens of them snatched right from their homes. You have saved so many children that you are now an honored pack member. Both you and your mate."

Aaron knew that she was overwhelmed. He was a little too. She was learning so much in so little time that he couldn't help but be impressed at her. But he knew that shortly he would want to kill her again. He wondered what would happen if he started carrying around a stake to threaten her with and dismissed the idea. He didn't need to have something so close at hand when dealing with her that she could, and more than likely would, use on him herself.

It took them nearly to sunrise to figure out the plan. It would have taken considerably less time if he hadn't had to keep reminding the twit that he was in charge every five minutes. Closing his eyes and pulling Sara to him Aaron wondered if Megan gave Beau this much trouble and decided he hoped so. Why should he be the only one to enjoy so much sarcasm and caustic wit? Aaron decided when this was all over he was going to write a book. He was going to call it *The Rules of the MacManus Realm*. He doubted that Megan would read it and, if she did, she would more than likely argue with him about every page.

~~~

Samuel was pissed. He didn't think he'd ever been so mad in…the nerve of that man telling him to come back tomorrow and then slamming the door in his face. He was going to make him pay. Right along with his master, the great and powerful Aaron MacManus.

Samuel went to his dungeon as soon as he returned to his home. He needed to hurt something, someone, and he knew that in the cells beneath his chambers there were plenty of someones he could hurt. He opened the door with his thoughts several feet before he got to the entrance. He liked it when they cringed, loved it when they scrambled away from him. This thing, a human, did both. Samuel wasted no time in playing, but picked the man up and threw him against the stone wall. The satisfying sound of his head hitting the wall made Samuel laugh. He tore from the room to go to the next.

Seven human deaths later, and he was still unsatisfied. He prowled around in the chambers wanting a new reaction, a new sound to come from them before he killed them, and it was always the same. He threw back his head and screamed at the injustice of it all, the unfairness of how the humans, even in death, could not do just one thing right. He made his way to the upper levels to find a female or two, hoping that during sex their deaths would bring him some happiness. But there was no one. Not one person was in the house. He searched everywhere, even in his own bedchamber, and found no one.

When he had searched every chamber, every closet, every small space he could think of, he finally went to his office. No one. There was no one in the house and he just knew that Aaron and that Megan had something to do with it.

"They took them away. Took my family, my kiss, away and have them hidden somewhere. When I have her power, power she stole from me, I'll kill that bastard and take them all back. I'll be the one that everyone runs to, the one that has the power."

Samuel looked around the room and wondered who had spoken. He got up and locked all the doors and closed all the curtains in the room. Not that anything could see in or out, the shades were down over these windows all the time. He never wanted to have even a small ray of sunlight enter this room or the ones he slept in. Samuel searched the room again. He was nearly through the room when he realized he had no idea what he was looking for. Making his way to the door he couldn't get it to open. Someone had locked it. Locked him in his chamber and wasn't letting him out.

It took him nearly an hour to remember that he had a key of his own and let himself out. He found himself in his labs before he remembered going there.

It was all set up. All the tests they'd done. All the results. All failures for the most part. Samuel pulled out another vial of the serum and tried to remember the last time he'd taken it. Was it four hours or four days? Had he already taken it or was this one in his hand the dose he was supposed to take? Samuel took the liquid into his mouth before he worked too hard at trying to solve the when of his medication.

The drug hit his system immediately. He calmed, his heart rate lowered, and he could feel his mind begin to sort things out, make order and sense of what he was thinking. After a few minutes Samuel could feel his skin fit his body again; the crawly feeling all over him dissipated and he could breathe easier. Soon after that he was himself again; reasonable, smart, and in control. Taking a deep breath Samuel felt embarrassed by his actions.

Samuel had tried to get Michael to tell him how the drugs worked. They weren't supposed to affect a vampire, nothing like that was. But he'd only smiled that smile of his and went on explaining things in terms he could neither understand nor remember. He looked around the room now and wondered what it all was. Beakers, test tubes, Bunsen burners and tubing—all of it there and all of it still.

The more the beast had taken control of Michael, the less was being done. Lately he'd begun working again, but it had only been in small spurts and not anything viable, he'd told Samuel. He wondered and got up to search again for notes that Michael had said he never kept.

Samuel sat on the floor after a few minutes of searching. He was exhausted from all the problems and the trials of being a master. He rubbed the area around his heart. It was giving him pains as if it wanted to hurt him too. He was sitting there when he saw the crooked stone in the floor.

Crawling over to it he tried to pry it loose. It was heavy and, before he realized he was going to need something else to work it loose, he'd bloodied his fingers and tore off his nails in the process. But he knew there was something there, just knew it. Getting up, he prowled around the room and found a bucket. Filling it with anything he could find to use as a tool he sat back down on the floor and began working.

Some of the things in the bucket were useless. Samuel wasn't sure why anyone would have given him such things to work with. But he didn't complain overly much, just tossed them away and grabbed something else. The pencil he was using had just snapped in two when he got up to get another vial of drugs.

"I don't know why you made the vials so small. I think next time you should...who's there?" Samuel stilled and looked around. "Michael? Creature? I don't like this game. Come here."

He ran across the room toward what he thought was a person and his head exploded in pain. He dropped to the floor and closed his eyes. Someone had hit him, he was sure.

Samuel found himself in the corner with two empty vials of the drug in his lap when he opened his eyes. He was alone, was the first thing he noticed, and he wondered where Michael had gone. He started to rise, but he was dizzy and his body felt...weird, he supposed was a good term. It took him several tries until he was finally able to leave the room. He decided to go to his chamber and rest. He wanted a woman, any woman, but couldn't remember where he'd put them. Sleep claimed him before he put too much effort into the search again.

Chapter 25

The plan was simple, they told her. Kill the master, take his power, and become the master of the realm. Too simple, Megan thought. So many things could and probably would go wrong. They had to sneak up on a man reputed to be over a thousand years old and then kill him without getting killed themselves. Megan looked at the men sitting at the table with her.

"You do know that this is not going to work. It's been my experience that—"

Aaron huffed at her. "And in your experience…how many years is that now? Fifty? Sixty? No, damn it, it's two. And not even that. Could you, I don't know, be a little less encouraging?"

She glared at him and Beau. She didn't like that he continued to laugh at her either. Oh he'd tried to cover it up with a cough or a sneeze, but after the first four times he'd done it she'd figured it out. Aaron just opened his mouth and she wanted to stake him. She eyed the wooden stake on the table and wondered.

"You touch that and I'll use it on you," Sara said from her right. "They are just men, you know. Simple is better for them. Less things to fuck up when it comes to crunch time."

Megan grinned. They'd been yelling at Sara too, Megan remembered. She wondered if Sara and she could come up with a plan that actually made sense, but dismissed the idea. Mel had

185

already told them that they couldn't use hers or Sara's magic to kill the master. The Council wouldn't approve of it.

Megan snorted. Sure, let the man kill her and whoever else went up against him, but hey, don't use the magic you have to save your ass! Stupid bureaucrats.

When they finally adjourned Megan looked at the map they had gotten. It showed the house that this Samuel person lived in. She hadn't understood the squiggly lines and the curly round things. Beau had told her they were bushes or trees. The place was huge. She could also see that there were all sorts of places for him to hide out men just to trap someone if he wanted to. She picked it up and looked at the area that had been marked "laboratory."

This area was bigger than her whole apartment when she'd had it. There were all kinds of areas in this that were marked with electrical outlets, stationary tables, and other things that she knew went into a lab. She kept studying it because she knew there was something there. Something they were all missing. Michael had given her his memories; wouldn't this include this room too? She was putting it down when she saw it. There in the corner of the room, one of those funny markings.

"Hey. Dingdong, come here and tell me what this thingy is. I think it might be a door or something."

Aaron came at her with his hands outstretched like he was ready to strangle her. She had pretty much ignored him because she knew that, while frustrated at her calling him that, she thought he kinda liked them sparring back and forth. She wouldn't admit it to him, but she did too.

"Megan, I swear to you that I will beat you myself when this is over. There are no doors in that ro…"

She leaned back when he got closer to the blueprint. He was moving his finger along the area where she had showed him then flipped the next sheet over to study it. That was another thing about this map. In order to read it, you had to go through seven hundred pages to get the "dynamics" of the room. A man invented this, she just knew it.

186

"I don't suppose you know what this could lead to, do you?"

She closed her eyes. They had been asking her to search her memories, or Michael's memories, for different parts of the whole for hours. "It's an opening to the outside. Some sort of hydraulic door, I think. It makes a noise, one that hurts his ears when it's opened. It's wide and...metal, steel. There is a tiny room to the right of it. It's reinforced rebar concrete and the beast can't...his claws only scrape it, but can't get much purchase when he tries to get at the man." Megan opened her eyes. "It's Samuel. He is...was afraid of the beast."

Aaron looked at her. He started to smile then it grew bigger until Megan was afraid of him. This was not a friendly smile, more of an "I'm going to eat you alive and enjoy it" smile. "Megan...do you know how to get into the building from here?" His voice was soft, but it made her shiver. She could only nod. Then it took her several tries before she could speak to him.

"There's a key pad on the outside. He'd, Samuel, had shown it to Michael once when they had been locked out. It's...it's... are you going to kill me?"

His fangs had dropped and his eyes had changed. Megan could feel Beau behind her, his hands resting on her shoulders. Low, menacing growls came from his mouth. His fingers were biting into her skin and for some reason she drew comfort from that. But it was the vampire in front of her that had her scared.

"No." She watched as he slowly regained control of...whatever he'd lost. "I'm sorry. I owe you an apology. I didn't mean to...I could see your memories. Or those of Michael about the room. Samuel needs to die. He cannot continue to kill our kind like he has."

Again, Megan nodded. She had them too, the memories, but she was trying to keep them in the back of her mind. It would do her no good to freak out because of what Samuel Rome had done to vampires. She needed to focus on the now.

~~~

Beau watched Megan wield the sword, practice with it she'd said. They were going out at just before dusk. Megan would be with him and the others were going to be close behind. They had tested several theories about her ability to withstand the sunlight, but Beau was still afraid for her. He wanted her to remain behind, but she wouldn't. Stubborn girl. And his attempts to put her into a deep sleep had only succeeded in pissing her off.

"*Mon amour*, could you not—"

"I swear, Beau, if you tell me you want me to stay once more I may use this thing on you. Removing your head might be a way to shut you up. I. Am. Going. End of conversation."

He wanted to growl, but the last time he'd done that to her she had growled back. It was a little terrifying to hear it come from her mouth, one that had only hours before had him deep inside of her. He shifted in the chair again as he thought of them in the lair.

She had told him she needed to rest. And he simply went with her to make sure she was alright. He'd stayed just long enough in the room to tell Aaron that he would be back soon. But he didn't make it back for several hours.

When he'd opened the door to their room she'd been naked. Naked and lying on the bed. His cock leapt to attention when she beckoned him to her. He moved like a man in a trance and then stopped when she stood up.

"I want to play, Beau. Would you be my willing playmate for a little while? I'll certainly make it worth your while." She ran her finger down his shirt and over the buttons. They scattered like the wind.

Taking his hand, she led him to the bed and pressed him down to it. He couldn't take his eyes off her. He wasn't even aware of anything until she was straddled over his legs. When he reached for her he realized that he was tied to the bed.

"Megan, let me go. I will touch you now." She shook her head. "This isn't funny, *mon amour*. Untie me from this bed." Looking over his head, he yanked as hard as he could, but couldn't get them to release. He turned to look at her and saw that she was grinning.

"Mel gave them to me. She said that I could use them on you and until I released you you'd be in my power. I think I like this." She leaned down and nipped at his nipple. "Just one more thing, then I'll play."

She settled between his legs and reached for the zipper of his pants. He didn't want to play, he wanted loose, but as soon as she licked the tip of his cock he decided he would let her play for a bit. He nearly came up off the bed when she took him deep in her mouth. Every part of his body came alive. He closed his eyes and let her have her way, not even looking up when she removed his pants. When she came back to his cock he tried to wrap his legs around her to hold her to him when he realized she had tied his legs to the bed as well.

"Megan, this is no longer amusing. You will let me go this minute. You have no right to tie me to the—Christ!"

Her mouth was on his balls, her tongue lapping at them. He couldn't even catch his breath when she started to roll them in her wet cavern. Beau felt his eyes roll to the back of his head and wondered if she planned to kill him. He decided that there couldn't be a better way to die.

Over and over she rolled him. Her small hand would brush against his cock, but she wouldn't take him. Twice he watched as her mouth skimmed over his thick head, but she wouldn't let him enter. Every time she got near him he would rock his hips up, trying to get his cock where it needed to be. But she evaded him.

He was hoarse from begging her. She ignored his every threat, his every plea for her to finish him. Every time he got close to coming, she would pull away and only tease him. He was going to kill her for this.

"I want to come on you Beau. Come as I ride you. Will you let me?"

He whimpered. He nodded. Hell, he'd sign his name in blood if she'd just let him be deep inside of her.

She moved her way up his body, nipping at his calf, kissing the small pain away. The back of his knees were tortured and laved with her tongue. When she got to his thigh, Beau wasn't above begging and nearly came up off the bed when she bit him there.

Her hot mouth suckled at the bite, his body on fire now for release. He knew the moment she touched him he was going to come. When she sealed the wound and rolled up his body, Beau knew that she was going to take him.

Her tongue flicked out and lapped the stream of cum off his cock. He watched as she circled his bulbous head and then took him into her mouth.

"*Mon amour*, please. Please finish me. Give me relief." He began rocking up into her. With every downward stroke he surged up. As he fucked her mouth her hand wrapped tightly around his shaft. He was close, so close his balls tightened and he could feel his cum racing up to spew. Then she stopped.

Beau pulled hard on the ties. He was going to have her and damn the bed. He snarled at her. "Take me. Finish me."

She moved up his body and impaled herself over him. Heat, scorching heat, grabbed him in a strangling fist and he surged up. Her hissed "release" gave him freedom.

Beau was beyond gentle. He wasn't even sure he could be less than savage. He roared at her as he grabbed her hips and yanked her hard down on him. Flipping her over onto her back he plowed her. Over and over he slammed into her. He showed her no mercy, only took.

Her channel grabbed him when she came, tightened around his cock so hard that he couldn't move for several seconds. When she screamed out his name he wrapped his arms beneath her and then over her shoulders from behind to hold her still while he punched his cock deep. He could feel her womb, feel her body tighten again and, when she clenched him, he threw back his head and poured himself deep into her body. Her bite, when it came, startled him. His cock, nearly spent, jerked again and spilled more of his seed deep.

Beau dropped. He couldn't have rolled off her if his life depended on it. When he heard her giggle, not a sound a man likes to hear after sex, especially sex like he'd just had, he raised his head and looked down at her.

"You will not think this so funny when I do the same to you, *l'amour de mon Coeur*. You nearly had me wishing for the sun."

She ran her hand down his cheek and over his chest to press against his heart. She held her hand there for a moment before she looked up at him and spoke. "I asked her for something to keep you safe, keep you here while I took care of that man. I was going to do it too until you came up behind me when Aaron scared me." She kissed his mouth gently. "I knew then that you would die getting loose. You'd kill yourself to come for me because you loved me."

Beau was brought back to the present by a small hand at his arm. He looked over at the little boy and smiled. Mac was such a serious little boy.

"I have a message for you. It's from your shadow, Michael. He said that you have conceived this night. He said that you need only listen to her heart and all would be well."

Beau stared at the little boy then looked over at his mate. Conceived. A child. He wanted to stand, take her to the bed, and tie her to it, but was stopped by Mac's next words.

"You can't do this alone, Mr. Beau. If you wish to succeed Michael said that you will need her with you to do so." Mac looked over at Megan too. "He said that she is the key to your well being."

Chapter 26

At three o'clock she and Beau were at the house. Beau had been acting strangely since they had risen, but Megan just thought it was nerves. She had them too. But he was acting like a maniac and she was ready to hit him.

"Beau, if you pick me up one more time to help me over a twig I will bash your head in. You're acting like a lunatic. Stop it."

He frowned at her. "I wish only to protect you. You cannot be harmed. It is my duty to keep you—"

"Duty smuty. Stop it or I will hurt you." She started forward again and he wrapped his arm around her waist. "Beau, you—"

"Shush…listen. Do you not hear that?"

She started to tell him no then she heard it too.

"Where are you? You are going to pay for this." It was Samuel; she'd know that voice anywhere. "I said that you will obey me and come out. Now."

Beau whispered through her mind. *"He is looking for us, oui? He knows of our plan."*

Megan grabbed his arm. No, that wasn't right. There was something off, something not quite right about his mutterings. They could see him now, not well, but they could see him coming across the field toward them.

"He's nuts. Or as close to it as they come. Listen to him, Beau. Listen to what he's saying."

"Michael? Come out, come out, wherever you are. I have to have that formula. And I don't like that you sent all my servants away. Did you know that there are seven hundred and fifty-three tiles on the bathroom wall? Who puts that—who's there?" He stopped suddenly then began dancing around the forest.

They watched him for another ten minutes before he was close enough to see clearly. He had changed, Megan realized. He was becoming his own kind of beast. His body was misshapen and he looked as if he'd lost weight. A great deal of it. Megan and Beau watched as he picked flowers only to destroy them, talked to the trees then try to scale them. Megan could almost feel sorry for him, but she knew what he'd done.

Then suddenly he changed again. He was there in front of them, mere inches from touching them.

"Hello, Megan. I have waited a long time for you." He reached out and grabbed her and tossed her behind him as Beau lunged for him. "She's mine and I'll have her."

Beau growled and attacked. Megan stood, but stopped herself from joining in. Beau wouldn't be able to fight if she was in the fray. Besides, she was slightly ill from the fall and wanted to get herself together before attempting to help.

The fight went on, over the field and skyward. Megan couldn't see every move; they were fighting at such dizzying speeds that all she could see were blurs and flashes of colors. Several times she thought that Beau had been tossed away, but before she could go to his aid he was moving back into the fight. When they stumbled toward her she gasped at the wounds on her mate.

He was torn to ribbons. His skin had open wounds around his face and along his arms. His belly looked to be bloodied and open, his hand holding over it. When she reached toward him he was jerked away from her by Samuel who laughed manically.

"I will kill him soon, Megan love. And when I do I will murder the child you carry and then fuck you until you die beneath me. I will have what is mine, have it all."

Child? Megan looked down at her flat belly. Child? She couldn't be pregnant, she was a...she looked at Beau and knew. He had known all night. Laying her hand over her child she called Beau to her.

"Feed. Take what you need and kill this fucker." She bared her throat to him and he didn't waste any time, but sank his fangs deep. Her body jerked from the sudden pain, but his arm wrapped around them and she felt his love. Samuel's rage could be heard echoing across to them. He didn't like that he was getting strength from her, enough, she was sure, to defeat him.

When Beau pulled away she turned and together they called the sword to them. When the pommel was clasped in their joined hands she let it go and nodded to him. Beau kissed her on the mouth and stepped around her toward Samuel. He didn't stand a chance.

The sword swung through the air like lightning. Each time it came down Beau hit another part of Samuel's body. His arm hung lank at his side. His head was bleeding from a wound at his temple. Over and over the blade arched over him, and over and over the man continued to rise. Then it hit her. He was drugged. He was taking the formula that Michael had invented.

Rushing to the door to the lab Megan opened it and went inside. It had been wrecked, all but destroyed. She knew it was Samuel; he'd been looking for something. She closed her eyes and waited for the memory. When it came she smiled. Going directly to the cubby hole in the floor she moved the stone and took out the vial that lay there. She realized that Samuel had been searching not four or five inches from where it lay.

Opening the door again she was surprised to find the two men had come this way. She knew that she had to make Samuel drink the drug and tried to think how to get it to him, then she thought of the children at the MacManus house.

"Beau, I have the drug. Take it and you'll be as strong as him. I'm going to toss it to you. Please catch it." She saw the men pause and hoped that she was correct. "Catch," she shouted before throwing it just to the left of Beau.

Samuel dove for it at the same moment that Beau did. Samuel snatched it out of the air and rolled until he came up on his feet. Megan nearly cried out in relief when he came up with it unbroken. She was sure the idiot would smash it in his attempt to get something that didn't belong to him.

He opened the little screw and held the tiny bottle up. "Here's to you, Megan. When I finish this pest off you and I will retire to my bed."

He downed the entire thing then threw the bottle at Beau. Megan held her breath and waited. When Samuel flew at Beau again she wanted to cry. Samuel seemed stronger than before, bigger and meaner. She dropped to her knees and sobbed. What had she done?

~~~

Beau lifted the sword and banged it against Samuel. That's all he'd been doing it seemed, banging away at a man who would kill him. Beau was exhausted and didn't know how much longer he could go on. And now Samuel's strength seemed to have grown exponentially since he'd taken whatever Megan had given him.

He knew what she'd done. He'd been in her mind since the moment that Samuel had appeared. He also knew that she wasn't really happy about him not telling her about the babe. He just hoped she got the opportunity to make him suffer for it. Then he noticed Samuel stagger.

The man seemed to be in pain. Beau drew up his weapon when Samuel doubled over screaming. When he fell to his knees and screamed again Beau stilled his sword, but held it at the ready.

When Samuel flopped to his back, jerking and convulsing, Beau looked at Megan. Tears in her eyes she smiled at him and he knew that it was going to be alright.

"It's the antidote," she whispered in his mind. "Michael hoped that the beast would find it and use it, but he never did. Then when the beast wouldn't use it Michael had hoped that he'd be able to, but he couldn't either."

"So this will kill him now." Beau watched her shake her head. *"Then what? I do not understand,* mon amour.*"*

"It will make him normal."

Beau looked at the man on the ground. Normal. Samuel would be just like any other vampire. He lifted his sword when Samuel rose.

"You can't fight me now. I'm not ready. You have to...I need to find something in the lab first. You can't expect me to win if I'm just like you. That's not fair." All he needed to do was to stomp his foot, Beau thought, and he'd have a hissy fit down. "You have to let me win, damn it. I deserve this."

Beau whipped the sword around and connected with Samuel's neck, then went through it. His head sailed across the forest tumbling over and over until it stopped against a tree. As soon as the head stopped rolling the body still lying in front of Beau exploded into ash. The head soon followed.

Beau dropped to the ground, his body spent. He managed to move the sword away before he impaled himself on it. Megan held him up before his face planted in the dirt.

"I'm exhausted, *mon amour*. I need rest. Take me to shelter and I will rest there."

"Oh no you don't, big boy. I need you to get up. I'm so not staying in this place until we get a serious cleaning crew to come in. That place is nasty."

He chuckled. Leave it to his mate to make him laugh at a time like this. Beau looked up when Aaron and his band of merry men, as Megan had called them, came into view.

"Ah, master. Now you show up? *Merde*, but the work, it is complete now." He tried to stand and found that he couldn't. "You will have to take my gratitude from here, sire. I find that I'm too..." He felt the ground kiss his face before he passed out.

Chapter 27

Aaron watched the man sleep. He'd been that way for nearly a week. He'd only just managed to get him and his mate to the mansion before the others, starving vampires and humans, came upon them. Beau was going to have his work cut out for him. Aaron knew the moment Megan returned to the house.

It was strange for Aaron to have a female child. Not of his blood, but of his bond. Megan had not been made by him, but the moment she came into his keeping without a maker she'd become his. He didn't mind nearly as much as he let on. She was a brilliant woman and he actually enjoyed sparring with her. But not even under threat of death would he tell her.

"How was your day? Did you manage to kill any unsuspecting people today?" He didn't even turn around when he spoke to her.

"No. Damn it. Why don't you come to the clinic tomorrow night and I'll see if you are filled with that gooey stuffing like your namesake is?" She flopped down in the chair beside him. "I hear Dingdongs are filled with sugar and lard...I can see the lard stuff, but sugar? Nope, not you."

They sat in companionable quiet for some time. The ticking of the clock was all the sound he could hear. He could feel her mind working and waited for her to speak.

"Aaron, that man, Samuel? He never believed I killed his child, did he? He was just trying to get you to give me to him."

Aaron waited. He knew she had more. "Why didn't you give me to him? You could have. It was well within your rights."

Aaron took her hand in his. "I've lived a great many years. Not all of them with family and friends around. And most of them in the pursuit of my next victim. I knew what Samuel was. I knew what he'd do to you if you were to go to him as well. At one time...well, that's for another time. I couldn't let him destroy you, Megan. Had I done that what would have become of my family? Of Beau here or of the others?"

She snorted. "Probably gone on to live a much happier life. You certainly are a mushy vampire, aren't you, King Dingdong?"

He growled at her. Damned girl, he really didn't know why she persisted in calling him Dingdong. And if it wasn't that, it was King Dingdong. Aaron smiled now. He'd had Duncan get him a package of them and had watched Sara eat them. Hummm, okay, maybe Megan calling him that wasn't so bad after all. She did introduce him to something Sara could eat and he could enjoy as much as a cheeseburger and fries. He sat up suddenly. Maybe Sara would enjoy a burger and then for dessert one of those creamy concoctions. He decided to find out.

"Your mate is resting easier now. He should rise soon. Oh, and the house you have acquired? It's ready for you. Good job getting it ready for him. He has a lot to do now that he's master."

Megan stood when he did. She looked...well, he was thinking uncertain, but that couldn't be right. He'd never met anyone more sure of herself than this girl. It bordered on arrogance at times. When she reached out and hugged him he suddenly knew that she was. He pulled her back and looked at her tears.

"Oh child, he will be fine. Beau has done this before and has been brilliant at it. You've nothing to worry about." He brushed away a tear. "Come now, if he wakes and finds you in my arms he'll be most displeased with me."

200

"He already is. Aaron, get away from my mate." They both turned to the bed when the man there growled at them. "Can I not leave you alone for ten minutes, *mon amour*, and you are in the arms of another? Come here, *femme de la mine*. I've a need for your body next to mine."

Aaron left the chamber when Megan told Beau that she was not his woman and he'd just better get that out of his vocabulary right now. He went in search of his own woman.

He found her in the nursery. She was asleep in the rocker that had been Mac's and Lizzy's when they were children. His son Daniel was awake at her breast. He was nursing again and Aaron touched his small head as he continued with his dinner.

"You are so precious to me. All of you. I would have met the sun by now had it not been for your mamma." Aaron spoke softly as he watched them. "I have so many things to be thankful for, my family mostly, and my friends. You, dear one, are the continuation of me and mine. You and your sister and brother will carry on where I will leave off."

"You going somewhere that I don't know about?" He looked up at Sara as she spoke. "If you are and think I'll let you, then you're are in for a staking, just so you know."

He kissed her gently on the mouth. "No, not leaving you. I have plenty more to do. Many more lives to touch. And I think I'm enjoying the ride. Are you?"

She kissed his mouth and stood up. When she walked to the crib and lay a now sleeping Daniel into it she turned back to him.

"Yes. I love to ride. The children are abed and the baby is fed. Why don't you let me show you how much I enjoy the ride?"

He stood when she reached out for his hand. He grinned. "Why don't I go down and see if there are any more of those chocolaty things from yesterday? I'm betting you'll need them before long."

"Oh, honey, way ahead of you. There's a brand new box right next to the bed."

Aaron was practically skipping down to their chamber.

About the Author

I woke up one morning and decided to give play time to the people in my head who were keeping me awake. Little did I know that they would be so relentless and want their time right now! I wrote for the pure joy of it and to entertain my family and friends. But mostly it was to get more than an hour of sleep without a story playing out. Of course, the more I write, the more they want. So…well, as a result of sleepless days (I work through the night as a gun toting grandma – nope not a vigilantly but an armed security guard) I have lots of stories written.

Hello! My name is Kathi Barton and I'm an author. I have been married to my very best friend Sonny for at times seems several lifetimes – in a good way, honey. And together we have three wonderful children and then the ones we brought into the world - Paul and Dale Barton, Jason and Wendy Barton and Danielle and Ben Conklin. They have given us seven of the greatest treasures on Earth. They don't live at home seven days a week! No, seriously, seven grandchildren – Gavin, Spring, Ben, Trinity, Sarah, Kelly and Kian.

Follow Kathi on her blog:
http://kathisbartonauthor.blogspot.com/